BACK TO VIETNAM

PENDLETON C. WALLACE

VICTORY PUBLISHING

Visit Pendelton Wallace's Web site at www.pennwallace.com

Contact the author at http://www.pennwallace.com/contact-penn.html.

Cover Design by Rebecca Poole

www.dreams2media.com

Vellum Formatting by Rick Lakin

BOOK I

GINO

THE BATTLE OF KHE SANH — SOUTH VIETNAM - FEBRUARY 1968

There are no atheists in foxholes. God, did Gino know that. He clutched the crucifix dangling around his neck and mumbled a *padre nuestro*. "*Padre nuestro que está en el Cielo.*"

Fear is that cold finger running down the spine. It's ice water in the veins. It's that sinking feeling when feet are frozen to the ground. The heart speeds up, lungs freeze. Hands and arms shake.

Bullets zinged past Gino's head and splatted into the foliage behind him. He wanted to run but where would he go?

Courage is facing and overcoming fear.

He looked up through the dense foliage at the gray sky. It had to be past noon. Not that it made any difference. The North Vietnamese Army often fought at night. And in this God-damned rain. The rain didn't come down in buckets. It didn't come down as cats and dogs. It was like being at the bottom of a waterfall.

After six years in this man's Army, Gino had faced tough situations before. But nothing like this. The whole God damned NVA perched just outside his spider hole.

"Taco Man, this is Liz-One, over." The voice of Captain Alan Albright came over the radio.

"Taco Man. Go ahead Liz."

"Pancho, new orders just came down." Albright's monotone showed the distaste he had giving the order. "You gotta hold your ground."

"Cap, I don't know if there's anyone else out here but me and Goober. I haven't heard any fire from the next hole in ages."

"I want to make this clear: Hold your ground." The captain paused. "To the last man."

Gino and Luther, his buddy from day one in boot camp, fought stubbornly on. Gino chose his targets carefully and used single-fire mode to take down his man. Goober went for automatic fire and hosed down the area. Torrential tropical rain obscured visibility. Gino couldn't tell if he saw a Gook or a palm tree. Bullets flew in their direction. They kept their heads down during periods of intense fire.

In the seconds when they were below ground, the NVA advanced to within one hundred yards of Gino's position.

"We ain't gonna get out of this, are we, Pancho?" Luther said as he slapped another magazine into his AK-47. A big man, he stood six-foot-nine and weighed nearly three hundred pounds. With ebony skin, he made an imposing figure.

Gino figured that if the NVAs just got a good look at his buddy, they'd turn and run.

"Hang in there, Goober. The cavalry is on its way." *Bullshit. All South Vietnam's gone to hell.* There was no help. Every fighting man in South Vietnam was already deployed.

Gino noticed movement in front of their hole. North Vietnamese regulars, the NVA. Lots of them. They were well-trained, well-disciplined, and well-armed. They didn't run when faced with opposition like the South Vietnamese troops. They held their ground and fought on.

Gino picked up his radio. "Fire base Liz, this is Taco Man, over."

"Go ahead, Pancho."

"We need artillery support." Gino gave the coordinates. "Pour down some fire on their asses."

Within minutes the roar of the big guns a mile behind Gino rent the air. High explosive shells rained down on the enemy. The forest exploded. Whole trees, bodies, and body parts flew through the air. Fire burst out everywhere despite the pouring rain. Some NVA soldiers fell to the ground. Sharp pieces of wood skewered the ones who didn't get down fast enough.

The hell rained down for what seemed like an immeasurable time.

Gino peeked over the top of his hole. Rain poured off his helmet. His feet were planted in three inches of mud and rainwater. He nervously rubbed the scar down the right side of his face from his hairline to his jaw.

There were targets galore as the North Vietnamese slowly regained their feet. Gino kept his AK-47 on single shot, much more accurate that way and it saved ammo, and picked a target. He gently squeezed the trigger. A dink jerked backward. Then another target and another.

Luther popped up and hosed down the recovering NVA troops.

"Careful with your ammo, Goober. There ain't no more where that came from."

Gino's head jerked violently to the right. He didn't hear the bullet coming. He just felt the impact on his helmet. He spun with the hit. A million bright lights filled his vision. Nausea and dizziness struck him. His head felt as if it had exploded. God how it hurt.

He crumpled to the bottom of the spider hole and sank into the water and mud. Luther dropped down and pulled off Gino's helmet.

"You okay, Pancho?" He gently checked his buddy for bullet wounds. Blood flowed liberally down Gino's face. "Nothing there, pard. But your helmet's a mess."

Luther held Gino's helmet in his hand and rotated it so Gino could see. Gino fingered the large gash down the right side. The sharp steel edges of the gash were covered in blood. Gino struggled to see. Everything was double.

"God damn." Gino reached for the helmet. "That was close." He bent back the sharp edges and plopped the helmet back on his head.

"You're one lucky son-of-a-bitch," Luther said.

Gino and Luther popped back up and resumed firing.

"I'm on my last clip," Luther said, as he loaded a new magazine.

"Me, too." Gino dropped the magazine out of his rifle and handed it to Luther. "You hold them off. I'll go for more ammo."

Gino slithered out the back of the hole. Bullets whizzed all around him. He kept his head down and crawled toward the next hole in the perimeter. The ground erupted around him as bullets plunked in the mud.

He looked over his shoulder. Luther was giving them hell.

Gino dropped into the next fighting hole. "*Jesus Cristo.*" Despite his double vision he made out two mangled bodies at the bottom. Dobbs was missing his head and Jenner's chest was full of small red holes. Gino rubbed his scar so hard he thought it might break open.

Gino checked their ammo belts. Both still had lots of ammo. They must have been taken out early. Like he and Luther, they used Chinese-made AK-47s instead of Army issue M-16s.

The AK-47 was a reliable weapon, and the ammo available everywhere. The M-16 jammed all the time and, even though the cartridges were much lighter and easier to carry, they could only get resupplied when a Huey dropped into the battlefield. He could pick up hundreds of rounds for the AK-47 off dead NVAs.

In Vietnam, the Army's Special Forces, the Green Berets, were law unto themselves. They chose what weapons they carried and what clothing they wore into battle. On some missions they dressed like Vietnamese peasants rather than elite U.S. soldiers.

Gino rubbed at the stubble on his face. Virtually all the Green Berets grew beards.

Loading himself down with all the ammo he could find, Gino made his way back to his hole.

"You're just in time, buddy," Luther said. He waved a Colt Model 1911 semi-automatic pistol in Gino's face. "I'm all out. All I got left is this pistol and my K-Bar."

"Here." Gino flung an ammo belt to this friend. "This should keep 'em occupied." He loaded a fresh magazine into his rifle.

"Geronimo," Luther screamed as he popped his head up and started firing.

It only took an instant for the bullet to find the big black man. He grabbed at his throat and fell backward into the hole.

"Christ," Gino yelled. He pulled Luther's hands away and surveyed the damage. Luther's throat was practically missing. He pulled a large sterile pad from his backpack and placed it over the gaping hole.

Luther's mouth moved, but only bubbly red blood came out.

"Here, keep the pressure on." Then he unwrapped a bandage and secured it around his friend's neck. He gave Luther a field injection of morphine. "That'll have to do until the doc gets here."

"Medic," Gino screamed into his radio. "We got wounded here."

There was no reply.

Gino sensed the enemy creeping closer. He got goosebumps on his skin. His heart rate soared. He popped up and hosed down the area. At least a dozen NVAs fell.

"Taco Man, this is Eagle Flight 1. We need a smoke bomb to locate our target," said the pilot of an F-4 Phantom jet roaring overhead.

"Roger that."

Gino grabbed a smoke grenade from Luther's belt. He pulled the pin and tossed it with all the force he had. Too close and he'd end up a crispy critter.

7

Moments after the red smoke lifted into the sky, the Phantoms came roaring over the battlefield. They dropped what looked like fifty-five-gallon oil drums. The drums tumbled end over end as they fell.

Then they hit. The jungle exploded into a maelstrom of fire, flames rising hundreds of feet into the air. Gino instantly smelled the sickly-sweet odor of burning flesh. He could see men, consumed in flames, running for their lives. They wouldn't make it. No one could survive a napalm attack.

The fight raged on all day. With nightfall, Gino got some relief. The enemy withdrew. *Thank God*, Gino thought.

He turned to his friend and checked for a pulse. There was none.

IN THE EARLY MORNING HOURS, two grunts fell into Gino's spider hole. Gino had never seen them before. They carried regulation M-16s.

"Cap'n wants to see you back at HQ," the spindly kid with a bad case of acne said.

Gino grunted and slithered out of the hole. He left the grunts to hold the position.

No shots echoed out. He clung to the mud and waited.

Silence filled the void. Not even animal sounds.

Gino crawled along the ground for a hundred feet before he came to trees to cover his retreat. He got to his feet and ran.

Firebase Liz was on a hill surrounded by trees. A bald spot on top of the hill was home to about two hundred GIs and Montagnard militia. The Montagnards were hill people. They lived in the 19th century in small villages made of bamboo hooches with thatched roofs. They hated the Communists.

A hundred yards past the tree line, razor wire covered the ground. Four MPs guarded the only entrance. Shell holes littered the ground surrounding the barbed wire. *It looks like the God damned apocalypse.*

Dozens of hooches, dug out of the ground, surrounded by sandbags, and topped with thatched roofs over steel plates lined the camp.

Each group stayed in their own hooch. Blacks in one. Whites in another. Several for Montagnards. A hooch for the Kit Carsons. One for the officers, another for warrant officers.

Three 155 mm guns and a 105 mm recoilless rifle were the primary weapons for the fire base. Half a dozen M-2 machine guns lined the perimeter.

In the center of the camp the four artillery pieces sat in silence. All of them had been taken out in the previous day's fighting. One 155 mm gun lay in pieces. The second had a bent barrel. The other had its wheels blown off making it impossible to aim. The recoilless rifle was a pile of junk.

The fire base had been through hell. Medics buzzed around wounded soldiers laid out in rows, waiting for evacuation, when choppers could get through the ground fire. The dead were behind the wounded.

Three-foot-deep shell holes pocked the once level road.

Liz was one of three firebases within spitting distance of the Laotian border. With interlocking fields of fire, they were supposed to control the area. *Shit,* Gino scoffed. *They're more a prison than a damned fortress.*

Gino's A-team was returning from a mission when they were pinned down in Liz. They were immediately assigned to the perimeter to keep the NVA from getting close to the base.

"Lookin' for Captain Albright," Gino said to the young corporal guarding the headquarters tent.

"Inside." The corporal stepped aside.

A tall thin man with sparse red hair, Albright was about five years older than Gino's twenty-three years.

"Sergeant Higuera reporting, sir." Gino was embarrassed by his own body odor. *I've seen better smelling gorillas.*

"Sit down, Higuera." The captain lifted a bottle off the desk and waved it toward Gino. "Need a wet?"

"Thank you, sir."

"Higuera, I know we've been in a hell of a fight." He handed Gino a glass. "Before sundown last night, choppers reported five or six thousand gooks surrounding our positions." He sipped from his own glass. "I need more intel. I want you to lead a recon patrol to see who's out there and what condition they're in."

Gino tasted the amber liquid in his glass. It burned good going down. *You're not my commanding officer. I can just make my way back to base and leave you jerks behind.*

"I know I can't order you to do this. You're MACV-SOG. Not under my command. But we're in a heck of a shitstorm here. I need intel and you're the man who can get it."

Oh shit. In for a penny, in for a pound. "Yes, sir."

"You can pick a squad to go with you."

"I'd prefer to take two Kit Carson's, sir." Gino held the captain's eyes.

"Kit Carsons? Can you trust those bastards?"

Kit Carsons were Vietnamese scouts. Most of them deserted from the NVA or the VC. They knew the territory and they hated the enemy.

"Yes, sir." Gino took another sip of his Scotch. "They're deserters. If the NVA captures them, they'll execute them on the spot. These sons-a-bitches are motivated."

Albright put down his glass and turned to a map on the wall. "All right. Intel puts large concentrations of NVA at these spots." He pointed to four positions surrounding the base. "I need to know if they're still there and their strength. I also want a body count."

Gino knew body count was how the brass could tell who was winning. *We kill more of them than they kill of us and it's a victory.*

Bullshit. The U.S. Army never held any territory. They could kill thousands of dinks and clear out an entire valley. As soon as the Americans withdrew, the land went back to the VC or the NVA.

It wasn't Gino's place to question orders, no matter how stupid. "Yes, sir. We'll leave at dark."

"Okay. Get back as soon as you can."

Gino saluted and turned to leave the tent.

"And, Higuera," the captain said to his back. "Make sure you get back. I need that intel."

GINO GOT TO THE KIT CARSONS' hooch and shouted out, "Four Eyes, Willie, on the double."

Two thin middle-aged men charged out of the dugout. "Sarge?" they said in badly accented English.

Both men were shorter than Gino, who was the shortest man in his A-team. *God damn. My team's all gone.* A wave of grief washed over him. He fought the urge to vomit. *Gotta get on with the job.*

"Okay, boys, we're goin' for a little walk." Gino wasn't used to giving orders to men twenty years older than himself. "Gather your gear. We leave at sunset."

The Vietnamese men turned without a word and hustled back into their hooch.

2

ESCAPE FROM KHE SAN — SOUTH VIETNAM

At dark, Gino and his two scouts headed out. They slunk past the opening in the razor wire and sprinted to the cover of trees two hundred yards away.

Inside the forest, Gino stopped to let his scouts catch their breath. Like Gino, they were armed with AK-47s.

Gino glanced back over the killing zone. *Keeee -rist*, he thought. The ground was littered with NVA bodies. He did a quick count. *Must be a couple hundred of them here.*

The buzzing of flies was overwhelming. After a day in the sun, the stench was nauseating. Dogs picked at the bodies. Vietnamese women and children had already stripped them of anything of value.

As they moved through the jungle, it was like a demon's dream. Trees were shattered, trunks and limbs littered the ground. In and under the mess lay another layer of corpses.

After a couple hundred feet, they came to the burned-out area. Smoke choked the air, and the odor of roasting flesh was everywhere. Small fires still dotted the waste-land. The charred remains of NVA soldiers were scattered about.

How the hell am I gonna get a body count? Gino rubbed his scar. *I can't count that high.* By then he was in the thousands. The NVA paid a heavy price for the assault.

The three men moved soundlessly though the hellish landscape. On the other side of the napalmed forest were hundreds of shell holes. What had been a beautiful tropical forest had been turned into a landscape of broken trees and dead animals. Once again, bodies and body parts littered the landscape.

They approached the first check-point. "Quiet," Gino whispered, although it wasn't needed.

He froze when he saw an NVA soldier standing guard over the hastily constructed camp. He pointed to Four Eyes and made a slashing motion at his own throat.

Four Eyes nodded and slipped silently forward. Using the jungle for cover, he moved around and behind the guard.

Gino lost track of Four Eyes. Then, out of nowhere, Four Eyes popped up behind the guard, put a hand over his mouth and slit his throat with a K-bar fighting knife.

Four Eyes lowered the soldier silently to the ground. Gino and Willie moved forward.

The camp consisted of hundreds of tents surrounding a makeshift road. Dozens of vehicles including armored cars and two Soviet T-37 tanks sat parked in the center. Three Soviet-made M46 130mm cannons rested in the midst of the other vehicles.

Armed troops made their regular rounds of the perimeter of the camp. The whole area buzzed with activity.

Shit. They're ready for another attack on Liz. Must be over a thousand troops here.

Gino took out his map and compass. He took bearings on two hills and marked where they crossed. That was his current location. He noted the coordinates to pass on to the artillery later.

Gino slowly led his scouts away from the camp and toward his second check-point. At each of the succeeding three checkpoints he found the same thing. Thousands of men, tanks, artillery, and support battalions.

Gino, Four Eyes and Willie made it back to firebase Liz in time to share the coordinates before the shelling started at dawn.

"MUST BE at least four thousand of the little bastards out there," Gino said.

A shell landed a couple of hundred feet away and shrapnel pounded the hooch.

"You say guns and tanks too?"

"That's right, sir. No way we can hold out here."

Captain Albright paced in front of the large wall map. "Jesus. With this cloud cover, no way we're going to get air support."

In the fight the day before, Albright lost his top NCO. He drafted Gino to fill the spot. There was no one else left from Gino's team anyway.

"We gotta bug out, sir." Gino said. He cradled a tin cup with lukewarm coffee in his hands.

"But how? We're surrounded by a force fifty times larger than us. How can we get through them?"

Gino sipped his coffee. *Disgusting. It tastes like mud.* "I think I can lead them through, sir. When we were scouting, we found a path that doesn't seem to be occupied. It cuts through the jungle down to this river here." He pointed to the spot on the map.

"HQ is sending two companies to get us out of here. They'll be cut to pieces by the NVA before they ever get here."

"Here, sir." Gino pointed to the map again. "If we can get them to rendezvous with us here, we should be able to sneak out."

THE TIRED MEN who survived fell in after dark. Gino took point and led them out of the razor wire encampment into the killing zone.

"Double time. March," Gino whispered to the man behind him. He waited a few seconds for the command to be passed back from soldier to soldier.

They carried only weapons and rations. All else was either destroyed or boobytrapped. Several smoke bombs were planted to let the soldiers know when the pursuit started. Their quick march bogged down in the mud from the previous day's rain. Insects made a holiday of it. No matter how much Deet Gino sprayed on, he couldn't keep the blood-sucking bastards at bay.

The men followed Gino's lead. They moved through the killing zone quickly into the cover of the dense jungle. Gino raised a clinched fist to signal them to slow down.

"Maximum quiet," Gino whispered. His order was passed back through the troops. The jungle noise disappeared. The sound of boots sucking in the mud the only sound heard. The fetid smells of rotting vegetation and feces filled the air.

With the Kit Carsons and Montagnard militia, the group had over 200 men. The soldiers carried five wounded men on stretchers.

A couple of hundred yards into the forest, Gino raised his fist to signal a stop. "I think I hear something. Willie, Four Eyes, go take a look."

The two scouts disappeared into the jungle. The company took deep breaths. Gino felt the fear that gripped most of the men. Good training held them together.

"Company size troops," Willie said when they got back. "Three, four hundred meters to west."

Captain Albright pondered the report. "Higuera, is there another way to your path?"

"I'm not sure, sir. We can send a scouting party east to see if there's a clear area." Gino's bullet-pocked helmet was lined with sweat. He removed the helmet and brushed back his damp black hair.

"Okay, get going," Albright said, with a slight tremor in his voice.

Gino led his scouts quietly through the jungle. They stopped often to listen. All was silent. No bird or monkey sounds. That was bad. *Must be dinks around somewhere.*

They encountered the first enemy patrol about a half hour into their recon. The three men froze and waited to see what the NVA were doing.

The five NVA troops moved through the jungle on alert, toward the American company. They made hardly a sound.

This is bad. Gino made a throat slashing motion to Willie and Four Eyes. Both men nodded. *If those commie bastards find us, we're done.*

They inched toward the patrol's path then lay in wait. The Vietnamese soldiers moved slowly forward. When the last man passed him, Gino leapt out, grabbed him and slashed his throat. Before the man ahead of him had time to react, Gino buried his knife in the man's throat. The next man in line spun and raised his rifle. Gino threw his knife and skewered the man in the chest. He was on top of him in an instant and cut his throat.

Willie and Four Eyes stood over the bodies of their victims. All returned to silence in the forest.

Did anyone hear anything? Gino signaled his men to freeze. He waited and listened for any disturbance. One minute. Two minutes. Three minutes.

Nothing happened. He stripped the bodies of ammo for their AK-47s then signaled his men to move forward.

When they got back to the company, Gino fought to suck in air.

"We moved east . . . then south for five klicks . . . sir." Gino raised a tired hand in salute as he came up to Captain Albright. "Encountered an NVA patrol and took them out. They were searchin' for us, sir. We gotta get moving."

"All right. Good work. Get us on the road."

Sergeant Higuera gave the orders and the men moved out.

Moving through the jungle in the dark was no easy thing. Especially when carrying five wounded men. With each bump in the road, they groaned or yelped.

"Silence in the line," Albright hissed.

Hours passed. The eastern sky lightened, pushing the darkness of night slowly away.

"Sir, I think we need to stop and rest for a while. Decide what we're gonna do next." Gino drank sparingly from his canteen.

Albright raised his hand, signaling a halt. "How far do you think we've come?"

"'Bout ten klicks." Gino wiped his brow. "We're still in the danger zone. NVA all around us."

"We'll rest up for an hour or so, then move on. Set pickets."

"Yes, sir. May I recommend we set up our machine guns on those little hills there?" Gino pointed to two small knobs on either side of their column.

"Yes."

While the men found places to sit or lie and the crews set up the machine guns, Gino took time to dig into an MRE. The food was cold and tasteless. It was just fuel for the machine.

Four Eyes and Willie sat next to Gino.

The air felt thick. Steam rose from the jungle floor where the rain evaporated. Gino had to breathe heavily to get a lungful, his shirt plastered to his body.

"Not good here." Willie said. "NVA not far off."

Gino nodded his head. "How far?"

"Maybe two klicks," Four Eyes said. "They ready to begin assault on base."

Good, that means they're not looking for us. "Okay, I'll tell the captain."

The company prepared to move out again. The first machine gun was broken down and the crew lined up for the march.

Gunfire ripped the air. Men fell. Others dropped out of line and found cover. The company returned fire.

"Holy God," Albright shouted. "Where the hell did they come from?"

Gino crawled behind a fallen log next to Albright. "It looks like a small patrol. They're trying to pin us down till the main force arrives."

"We can't stay here and wait for that." Bullets thumped into the log.

"I'll get that last machine gun on them. We'll hold them. You get the men moving."

Without waiting for a reply, Gino slithered toward the hummock where the last machine gun was located. "Willie, Four Eyes, flank me."

The three men made it safely to the gun. "You guys get your asses outta here," Gino said to the gun crew. "Me and the Kit Carsons'll hold 'em till you're safe."

The gun crew scampered down the back side of the hill.

Gino took the gun and Four Eyes loaded for him.

As he saw movement in the jungle, he laid down fire in their flank. Gino saw several bodies splayed on the ground where he had just fired.

Gino could see the NVA regroup and prepare for an assault on the machine gun.

"Willie, move out to the left. Find a good position, then take those bastards out."

Willie nodded, cocked his AK-47, and disappeared into the jungle.

The NVA moved cautiously forward. Gino opened fire. He couldn't tell if he had done any good or not.

He saw movement on his right. Before he had the chance to swing the big gun, a pistol shot rang out. An NVA soldier dropped to the ground. Four Eyes twirled his Colt .45 semi-automatic pistol around his finger like an Old West gunfighter.

"Fastest gun in West." He smiled.

Gino turned his attention to the attacking patrol. They cautiously made their way up the hill.

Gun shots rang out from the left. Two soldiers fell. The men immediately turned to the source of fire.

They ignored Gino for an instant and moved toward Willie. Gino laid down a spray of bullets and dropped another two men.

The NVA patrol was caught in a crossfire. Their commander ordered a withdrawal. They continued to pepper Gino's position as they slunk back into the jungle. Finally, they were out of range. Gino took the time to look for his retreating company. They were nowhere to be seen.

"Bastards pulling out," Willie said as he rejoined Gino and Four Eyes.

"Yeah, but are they returning home or following our guys?" Gino made an instant decision. "We gotta go after them. Leave the MG behind and let's move."

He picked up his rifle and hurried down the slope, the two scouts keeping pace.

Gino set a bruising pace as he moved through the forest. He had to find those fuckers before they led their main force back to his men.

Willie and Four Eyes were expert trackers. They found the spoor of the retreating patrol and stuck to it.

In about ten minutes, they heard soft voices ahead of them.

Gino held up his hand and listened.

"Lieutenant telling men to hurry up. Must get back to camp," Four Eyes translated.

"We gotta get ahead of 'em and set a trap." Gino moved off to the left.

There were a few animal trails through the jungle. Gino and his men moved like wraiths through the forest at break-neck speed.

Eventually Gino thought they'd gone far enough. He sent his scouts to the other side of the game trail the enemy followed and made himself invisible in the bushes.

A point man was the first to show up. He wore a North Vietnamese uniform with tree branches strapped to his back. All the NVA did the tree branches thing. If attacked, they could drop into the jungle floor and become invisible.

Gino let the point man pass. He was followed by a young lieutenant and seven men. A drag man was a hundred meters behind them.

As the lieutenant came opposite him, Gino opened fire. The lieutenant went down. The scouts on the other side of the patch cut down three more NVAs before they could react.

The remaining five men scrambled for cover returning fire. Bullets buzzed around Gino's head like of a swarm of bees.

The scouts from across the path took out another NVA soldier. Gino laid down a pattern of fire hitting another man. There were three NVA left.

Gino couldn't see his men across the path but knew they were experienced fighters. A shot rang out as the point man dashed back to his comrades. He tumbled ass over tea kettle and came to a rest by the side of the path.

Two more.

From nowhere, Willie popped up right next to the NVA soldiers' cover and hosed them down.

"All clear?" Gino asked as he cautiously rose from his position.

"We good," Willie replied.

They searched the bodies and found a packet of papers in the lieutenant's pocket. Neither of the scouts could read and Gino had no knowledge of Vietnamese, so he pocketed the papers, stripped the bodies of ammo, and moved out.

They followed the company's trail for an hour before catching up.

The GIs moved through the jungle as quietly as possible, but Gino heard them a hundred yards away.

A burst of small arms fire split the air. Gino heard the captain shouting and men dashing for cover.

The enemy paid no attention to Gino and his scouts at their rear.

Four Eyes held up all his fingers, closed his hands into fist, then held up ten fingers again.

Twenty of the little bastards. Gino gestured to his men, and they moved closer and found cover. Gino dropped an NVA with his first shot. Willie and Four Eyes were equally efficient. They downed five or six men before the enemy even realized they were there.

Gino saw movement in the bushes beyond the enemy patrol. *Good for Albright. The son-of-a-bitch is smarter than he looks.*

Gunfire blasted from the Army position. The crossfire caught the NVA off guard. Men died. The commander tried to rally his men and retreat, but his head exploded in a mass of blood and brains.

The fight only lasted about fifteen minutes but to Gino it felt like a lifetime.

When he and his scouts joined the company, they learned that there were no American casualties.

"God damn," Albright said. "We got lucky. Good thing you showed up when you did."

Gino sat on a downed log and reached for his nearly empty canteen. "How're the men doing, sir?"

"They're too tired and hungry to be scared. We're running low on ammunition." Albright removed his helmet and wiped his forehead.

"We gotta keep movin', sir. The Gooks can't be far off." Gino's clothes stuck to his body, soaked with sweat. He smelled like a gym locker room.

They traversed the forest floor and came to the river at sundown. Albright radioed the rescue force and set a time and place for the rendezvous.

Gino kept them moving through the night and on the third morning they came upon pickets from the two companies. In the early morning light, they cleared a landing zone. In a short time, a flight of Hueys, UH-1 Iroquois helicopters, settled unto the LZ and lifted the men out.

This sure as fuck was a losing battle. Even though Gino had counted more than a thousand NVA bodies and the Army had lost only sixty-three dead and fifty-six wounded, they fought their way out with their tails between their legs.

The brass will report this as a great victory.

"Higuera," Captain Albright said, "I want you to know that I'm recommending you for the Congressional Medal of Honor."

3

LEAVING MEXICO — CHIHUAHUA, MEXICO

Sixteen-year-old Gino Higuera stood and stretched his back. Tomato bushes with bright red fruit surrounded him. Wooden boxes lay on the ground. He couldn't remember how many he filled that day.

Papa farmed a few acres of dusty land a few kilometers north of Chihuahua city. Gino rose early every morning to feed the goats and chickens. His six younger siblings all had their own chores.

"Mijo," Papa shouted in Spanish. "Put your box down. It's time to get dinner."

Gino didn't know if he was happy or sad. Picking tomatoes was back-breaking work but chasing down rabbits was exhausting.

He met his father and two uncles by the well. While they got ready, he glugged down two ladles of water. It was bitter and gritty.

Papa and his uncles Tino and Martín carried long, sharp sticks. Papa handed one to Gino. The four men took off at a trot toward the fields.

"Aiee. There's one," Martín shouted.

The men changed course and sprinted toward the fat rabbit. The rabbit took off.

"Keep him in sight," Papa called.

Gino took the extreme left side. If the rabbit turned his way, it was his job to herd it back to the center.

That little bastard can run. Gino panted for breath as the chase continued. It was a contest of who was going to run out of gas first, the rabbit or the men.

Papa had by far the most stamina of the four. He could run for hours in pursuit of game. Gino was new to this and struggled to keep up.

How far had they chased the beast? Maybe a kilometer, maybe two. The rabbit showed signs of wearing down. It stumbled, then got up and ran again. Gino could see its sides going in and out as it struggled for breath.

Then it happened. The rabbit stopped. Tino was the first there. He speared the rabbit and held it up. "Ay, Chihuahua. That was a fast one." He dropped the rabbit into a white flour sack attached to his belt.

The men repeated the process three times before the darkness bid them return home.

The men gave the rabbits to Mama and his sister Angelina. Gino collapsed on his bed.

I've gotta get outta here. There's no future in Chihuahua.

Unlike many of the other children in the dirt-poor farms surrounding the big city, Gino did not go to school. The school was free, but the parents had to buy the uniforms and the books. There was no money for him. Besides, Papa needed his labor on the farm. By the time his youngest brother, Eduardo, was old enough, Papa scrapped together the money to send him to school.

This is it. I'm done here. I'm going to America.

TIJUANA WAS A BIG CITY. Everything was fast and flashy. For a farm boy like Gino, it was another world.

He found a job washing dishes in a big restaurant and found a room he shared with two other boys. He worked the night shift, so they slept in the two beds at night. When he got home, they got up and went to work. Then he had a bed to himself.

"I'm sorry, Patron," Gino said to his boss. "This is my last night. I leave for America tomorrow."

"Humph." The fat man brushed at his mustache. "I supposed you're going to want to get paid tonight?"

"*Si, por favor,*" Gino replied.

At the end of the shift, he collected his pay and returned to his room. It was still dark. Gino grabbed his already packed backpack and headed out the door. He knew just where he was going.

The one-story factory building had a corrugated iron roof. Gino climbed the wrought iron bars over the door and made his way to the roof. He glanced about to see if anyone watched.

The town was sleeping. He made his way to the edge of the roof.

Below he saw the red metal wall between Mexico and the United States. He didn't stop to think. He just took a deep breath, ran, and jumped.

In the second or two it took him to reach the ground, time slowed down. He hung in the air and thought. *This is it, compadre. We're really doing it.*

He hit the ground and rolled. *Jesus, Jose, y Santa Maria. I'm in America.*

It didn't last long. Before he had gone three blocks, a white SUV with a shield on the door and writing Gino couldn't understand, pulled up with red lights flashing.

Caca, migras. Immigration cops.

Two middle aged Mexican-American men popped out of the doors.

"Hold it right there, son," one of them said in Spanish, as he pulled a large revolver. "Put your hands up."

By daylight, he was on a bus headed back into Mexico. They dropped him off in the central plaza and he immediately made his way back to the small factory building.

He was back in America before noon. This time he ran. Using the stamina he built up chasing rabbits, he ran through the streets and open fields until he couldn't run anymore. He was maybe five kilometers from the border. He found a depression in the ground surrounded with yellowing grass. He dropped in and fell asleep.

"THIS IS GOOD," he told the driver of the eighteen-wheeler in Spanish. "My cousin lives near here."

The truck took the next off ramp from I-5 and left Gino standing on the side of the road. He walked toward town and stuck out his thumb at every car that passed.

"Gino," his cousin Jose exclaimed when he opened the door. "You made good time."

"I got a ride with a long-haul trucker, and we came straight through."

Gino showered and shaved, then sat down to dinner with Jose and his wife, Estella. He slept on the couch and awoke before daylight when Jose shook his shoulder.

"Time to get up, *huevon*. Gotta be in the fields by daybreak."

The field work in Fresno was just as back-breaking as working in his father's fields in Mexico, only the money was better. This was just a start. He needed to get his feet on the ground and learn a little English before he moved on.

While he worked the fields during the day, he attended adult education classes at night. The English came easily and soon he was reading English as well.

When winter came, he had saved a little money and was ready to move on.

L.A., that's where everything is happening.
So, he hitched to L.A.

THE JOB WASHING dishes in a greasy-spoon restaurant was awful. He hated the work and hated the boss. The waitresses weren't bad.

Rosa was twenty-two, a little heavy, had deep-brown eyes like chocolate pools, and had *chi chis*. My God, she had *chi chis*. Gino couldn't look her in the eye. Several times she said, "Hey, Chango, I'm up here," and pointed to her eyes.

Gino was so embarrassed he couldn't reply.

She teased him incessantly. *She must like me to spend so much time picking on me.*

But that's as far as it got. Gino had no real experience with women. He knew his sisters, but that was different. This was far more serious.

"Hey, Changito, what you doin' after work?" Rosa asked.

Gino dropped his dish towel and stared at her as if she were a twenty-ton truck bearing down on him.

"Uh . . . I don't . . . I not doin' anything." He tried to use English as much as he could. It was coming along nicely.

She rubbed up against him as she walked by. "Well, when are you going to ask me out?"

"I . . . uh . . . I mean . . . *Caca*, how 'bout now?"

"I get off at nine."

"Me not til eleven." His head hung low. He knew he missed his chance.

"Good. It'll give me time to go home, shower, and change. I'll meet you at *El Monterrey*. Say eleven."

"Uh . . . Okay. Sure."

He didn't know where the rest of the night went. Before he knew it, he was running up the street to the bar Rosa mentioned.

He was underage but looked older. *I wonder if Rosa knows how old I am? Nah, it don't matter. I'm man enough for her.*

Brave thoughts for a boy who had never been with a woman.

He sat at the bar and sipped a *Dos Equis*. The bartender didn't ask for his ID.

Rosa entered the bar like a queen. She wore a short, tight, black skirt and white go-go boots. With the top three buttons of her white blouse unbuttoned, she bulged out of the opening.

Rosa flipped her small black purse onto the bar and took the seat next to Gino. "This seat taken, Chango?"

Gino stared open-mouthed at her. He'd never seen such a vision before.

She gently touched his jaw and closed his mouth for him. "What, you never seen a real woman before?"

"Na . . . No . . . I mean yes. I've seen lots of women. But, ah . . . . never dressed like that. I mean, I seen 'em in movies and stuff, but never anyone I know."

"Well, get used to it, amigo. I think we're gonna be seein' a lot of each other."

Rosa lived with her parents, so after a couple of beers, Gino led her to his room in a cheap hotel.

"Wow. You're sure livin' the life of luxury, aren't ya?" Rosa said as she stepped through the door.

The room was less than spectacular. An old, steel-framed double bed sat against the wall. A tiny round table with two unmatched chairs pushed against the window. A pine dresser and a miniature black and white television set finished the décor.

The view out the window was spectacular. The room looked down on a parking lot, a freeway bridge, and an abandoned warehouse building.

Gino felt his face flush.

"Come 'ere," Rosa said and grabbed Gino by the collar. She led him to the bed and plopped down. "Come to Mama."

Gino just stood and stared.

Rosie unbuckled his jeans and dropped them and his underwear to the floor. Gino was already hard.

She took him in her hands and began to pump.

Gino was out of his mind. Memories of every dirty movie he ever watched flashed through his head.

Rosa took him into her mouth and started to suck.

He came right away.

"My goodness," she said as she wiped her mouth. "You're mighty fast."

"I uh . . . I mean . . ."

"Don't worry about it." Rosa unbuttoned her blouse and let it fall to the bed.

Gino's eyes popped. She was wearing a black lacy bra that left little to the imagination.

Rosa unzipped her skirt and wiggled out.

Her panties matched the bra.

She pulled Gino's T-shirt over his head and massaged his hard pecs and ran her hands down his rock-like abs. "My goodness, Chango, you got one bad-ass body, don't you?"

He didn't reply. He sat on the bed next to her, nude. He reached over and pulled her head toward him.

The kiss was like none he ever had. He'd kissed his mama and sisters from time to time, but that was a whole different animal.

He tasted her soft ruby lips. Her tongue flicked in his mouth. He inhaled a deep breath. He could feel the throbbing in his penis.

She put both hands around his neck and forced him to the bed. He felt the weight of her pushing on him. He refused to break contact with her lips.

She reached behind her back and unsnapped her bra. Her giant *chi chis* fell free. Gino reached up and took one in each hand. They were wonderful. They were soft and spongy. He squeezed them and they popped out of his hands.

He ran his hands along her sides. He couldn't believe the softness and smoothness of her body. He caressed her hips and ran his hands from her waist to her hips repeatedly. She was incredible.

She pushed him back on the bed, pulled off her panties and climbed on top of him.

He felt the heels of her boots bite into his legs.

She took him in her hand and put him inside of her.

Gino's world exploded. He never imagined anything like this. It was nothing like when he jacked off.

She worked her hips and slid up and down on his penis. Her breathing was loud and erratic. He grabbed her hips and held on.

She leaned forward and her breast grazed his chest. He took in a deep, sudden breath. *Dios mio.* Never in his wildest dreams had he ever thought it would be like this.

He grew up on a farm. They had animals. He had watched the animals mate, but never imagined what it would feel like for him.

She screamed and dug her fingernails into his shoulders. "Watch me come, watch me come," she shouted.

Her face crinkled up. She closed her eyes and knitted her eyebrows. She sucked her cheeks in. Her lips pursed out like a puffer fish. She shouted, "Fuck me, fuck me," then let out a huge breath.

He came immediately. He felt the tingle in the soles of his feet. He felt fire move up his legs. He penis erupted. He felt the hot fluid flow out of him.

She gasped and pulled herself close to his chest. She breathed deeply and tears fell from her eyes.

He was spent. He lay there taking her weight on him. He softly ran his hands over her back.

When he woke in the morning, she was gone.

4

THE MEAN STREETS OF L.A. –
LOS ANGELES, CA

Gino walked down the aged hallway for a shower and shave. Afterwards, he dressed in black pegged jeans and a white T-shirt.

The streets of L.A. were a marvel to him. So much humanity flowed past. Shops of every kind with plate-glass windows displayed their wares. He stopped in front of an electronics store and marveled at the color TV consoles in the window.

Someday, I'm gonna have me one a them.

He turned the corner and was confronted by three boys. They were about his age, all Mexicans. The tall, thin one with a scar across his brow held up a hand.

"Hey, *babaso*, what you doin' on our territory?"

Gino froze. "Your territory?"

"That's right, *pendejo*, you walk our streets, you gotta pay the tax."

Gino slowly came to his senses. "Tax?"

"Whatcha got on ya, asshole?"

Two other boys grabbed Gino from behind. He struggled to break free. The spokesman hit him hard in the belly.

He breath whooshed out from him.

The leader landed a few blows to his face.

Gino slumped in his captors' arms. They let him fall to the ground.

All three boys kicked him.

The tall boy searched Gino's pockets. He had twenty-three dollars and seventeen cents. He had just been paid.

"That's your tax, *pendejo*."

The world went black.

EVERY BONE in Gino's body hurt. He slowly opened a swollen eye. Everything was blurry.

"Welcome back to the world of the living." It was a female voice.

He felt a warm cloth applied to his brow. It carefully wiped out his eyes.

He blinked. He could open both eyes.

He looked up at Rosa, tenderly wiping the blood off his face.

"You sure took a beating, Chango."

"Mmmm . . ."

"For a smart guy, you sure don't have any street smarts." She tenderly kissed his forehead. "I'm gonna set you up with my cousin. He'll protect you."

ROSA'S COUSIN Danny was a small, wiry young man. Gino thought he might be four or five years older than himself. He had a go-to-hell, Clark Gable mustache and wore flashy clothes.

"So, Rosa tells me you got beat up by the *Chulos*?"

Gino nodded.

They sat in a back booth at *El Monterrey*. Ranchero music

blasted from the speakers. Gino thought his head would blow up. It took all he had in him to walk the five blocks from his room. He was exhausted.

"Hey, man, you don't belong to a gang around here, you nothin'." Danny took a long drag from his Corona bottle. "I can get you fixed up. You gotta swear the oath and do the initiation and you in." He flipped the sleeve of Gino's T-shirt. "Man, we gotta get you some threads. You look like you just got offa the boat."

The gang met in an abandoned warehouse. Broken glass from the windows littered the floor. They sat on old cable spools, a couple of dilapidated sofas, and an assortment of lawn chairs. A large cooler with beer on ice made for a table in the center of the space.

"You think this *Chulo* got what it takes?" His mother named him Benjamin, but his street name was Tiburon, the shark. The leader of the *Santa Muertes* was the biggest bastard Gino had ever met. He had huge shoulders and a giant barrel chest. His arms looked like he could pick up a car.

"He's new bro." Danny answered. "He's only been here a few months. But he's strong and smart."

Tiburon walked slowly around Gino, who stood still in the middle of the circle. "You gotta do an initiation, *Chulo*. Let me see . . . yeah. You gonna find Juan del Gado and pay him back for this beatin'. No one picks on a *Muerte*. I'll send a couple of guys to back you up, but you gotta do it."

"You gotta be careful, *compadre,*" Danny said. "He's one mean son-of-a-bitch."

Gino just stood there, saying nothing. *Who the hell are these guys? And they want me to beat up that tall bastard?*

"Okay," Tiburon said. "Then I think you're gonna bring Rosa back here and fuck her while we're all watchin'."

GINO PUT Juan del Gado in the hospital. Then he brought Rosa to the hangout. They fucked on an old, stained mattress. The other boys pissed on them while they fucked. The girls hiked up their skirts, squatted over them, and did the same.

The gang started to trust him. They started him as a runner. He delivered drugs to the pushers on the street corners. It was a dangerous job. Rival gangs loved to intercept *Los Muertes* shipments and disrupt their business. He fought his way out of several tough situations.

The cops watched for runners. They wanted to catch 'em and flip 'em.

Gino knew that talking to the cops was signing his own death warrant.

First, he got a better room. Then, when they promoted him to his own street corner, he rented an apartment. Rosa moved in with him.

The money started to flow. The first of every month he went to the Western Union office and wired money to Papa. He started to stash some cash in a secret hiding place under the floor in his bathroom.

Then came the car. All the *hermanos* drove low-riders. Gino found a Chevy Impala with leather seats and a custom paint job.

Life was good.

GINO STOOD in the doorway of a closed shoe store on his corner. His long black hair and wannabe mustache marked him as a street kid. His dark eyes burned with desire.

Gomez was a regular. At least twice a week he found Gino on his corner. Money changed hands, and Gino gave Gomez a little packet filled with white powder.

That day was no different.

"Hey, man, I need a hit," Gomez said. His eyes were bulging, and he sweat profusely.

He was about Gino's height, but thin as a string. His hands shook as he handed Gino the money.

"Your life, *menzo*," Gino said as he dug in the oversized pocket of his oversized GI surplus jacket. He handed the packet to Gomez.

"Freeze. LAPD." The voice came from somewhere behind him.

In an instant, two cops in plain clothes and two uniformed troopers converged on him.

"*Mierda,*" Gino shouted and ran. He was fast and he had endurance.

The uniformed cops chased him. The other two ran for their car.

Gino turned a corner and dashed into an alley.

He emptied his pockets as he ran.

"Stop. Stop or we'll shoot," the older cop yelled as he fell behind.

Gino looked over his shoulder and grinned, then crashed through a doorway and ran through a building. He was in the kitchen of a Mexican restaurant. He fled into the dining room, then out the front door.

The cops followed, both of them winded.

Gino smiled. He'd leave them behind. When he crashed out into the street he ran right into a police car. Before he had a chance to change direction, the undercover cops in the car jumped out and grabbed his arms.

"Hold it right there, wetback," the big cop said. He forced Gino to turn to the car and put his hands on the roof. "Spread 'em." He used his feet to kick Gino's feet apart.

The second cop patted Gino down, then slapped cuffs on him.

The two cops who chased Gino arrived on the scene, breathing hard. The older of the two bent forward and put his hands on his knees to catch his breath.

"Think you can get away from us, you stupid beaner." The first cop that chased him pounded a fist into his kidneys.

Gino gasped and sunk to his knees.

The second cop who chased him pulled his billy club from his belt. "You wetbacks have to learn a lesson." He pounded Gino around the head and shoulders.

Gino slunk to the pavement.

The cops kicked him until he passed out.

"AUGUSTIN HIGUERA, you have pled guilty to drug trafficking." The judge was a thin middle-aged man with a Roman nose, losing his hair. "I see that your attorney and the people have reached an agreement as to your sentence."

Gino stood behind the defendant's table with his court-appointed lawyer by his side. He held his head down in shame. *If Mama could see me.* A reluctant tear rolled down his cheek.

"Based on that agreement, you have a choice." The judge's voice carried all the gravitas of the situation. "You will be sentenced to five to seven years in a state penitentiary. At the end of your sentence, you will be deported back to Mexico."

Gino gasped. Seven years. *That's a lifetime.*

"Or," the judge let the word hang in the air, "you can join the U.S. Army and start giving back to this country."

That was no choice at all. In a matter of days Gino was shipped off to boot camp to wear olive green.

5

OPERATION IVORY COAST - IN THE AIR OVER NORTH VIETNAM NOVEMBER 21ST, 1968

Gino led his A-team onto the HH3-E Jolly Green Giant helicopter just before 0200 hours at the Udon Air Force Base in Thailand. They were in the air by 0218.

The men were lost in their own thoughts. Visions of family, girlfriends or wives, places dearly remembered floated through their minds.

Each of the fourteen men knew they were going into combat. They knew that their objective was deep inside North Vietnam. They knew if they failed, there was no coming back.

The thumping of the helicopter blades drowned out all chance of conversation. Gino took his crucifix in hand and said a *padre nuestro*. Outside the windows, dense clouds obscured the view.

"Lime One, this is Banana One. We're at checkpoint one," a voice came over Gino's headset. "Too much cloud to refuel. We'll climb out of the clouds to find you."

"Roger that, Banana."

The big helicopter rose, and Gino's stomach fell. They broke out of the clouds at seven thousand feet. An HC-130P Combat King tanker circled, waiting for them.

For the next fifteen minutes they took on fuel then headed farther north. Gino's heart rate climbed. They were over North Vietnam. Enemy territory.

Thump-thump-thump. It seemed a lifetime, then a voice came over the headset. "Decoy landing site in five minutes. Get ready, boys."

A soft voice came over the intercom in broken English. "Have you in sight, Banana."

"Roger that. Are we cleared to land?"

"Look good. No NVA around."

The big chopper swooped down into the clearing and hovered six feet off the ground. The Green Berets inside pushed uniformed dummies out the cargo ramp.

The chopper climbed and moved on to the next location.

After three more decoy landings, the pilot's voices came on. "Okay, boys get ready. We're five minutes out to our real landing site."

"Banana One, Scout One."

"Go ahead Scout One."

Gino recognized the voice. Four Eyes.

"LZ clear. No sign of enemy."

Where do they get men like these? They know that the chopper is going in, but it ain't comin' back.

According to the plan, twenty A-7 Corsairs and A-6 Intruders launched from off-shore carriers nearly an hour earlier. If all was going well, the largest night raid of the war was pounding Haiphong Harbor. Gino crossed his fingers. *Please, God, let them be right.*

If the operation went according to plan all North Vietnam's attention was diverted to Haiphong. No one would notice a flight of Jolly Green Giants and their escorts swooping into the valleys like giant insects as they flew toward Hanoi.

After two hours and twenty-six minutes of flight time, the choppers reached their target within thirty seconds of the plan.

"Here we go, boys," the pilot said. "Rig for crash landing."

The air around the compound exploded as gunships blasted the guards' barracks and the watch towers.

The prison compound at Son Tay was too small for a regular landing. The big bird came in hot, crash landing in the center of the compound.

"Banana One is on the ground," the pilot said.

Gino was first out the door. His Green Berets exited the helicopter and formed a perimeter around the downed bird. Then they moved forward toward the barracks.

Captain Meadows raised his bull-horn. "We are Americans. Keep down. We're here to get you out."

There was no response.

Small-arms fire and explosions erupted outside the compound. The second combat group attacked as planned. Gino motioned his team forward. They cautiously went from building to building. All empty.

A few NVA soldiers ran from burning barracks and were taken out immediately. The gunships roared overhead.

There were several NVAs in the admin building. The Green Berets neutralized them.

"Cap'n," Gino saluted as he reported. "There's no one here. The prison cells are all empty."

"God damn, son of a bitch." The captain was not one who normally took to purple language. "Where could they be?"

"Don't know, sir. But I'm thinkin' we should withdraw."

The soldiers made their way out of the camp and joined up with the two combat teams outside.

The Jolly Green Giants swooped in and lifted the troopers out of the camp. They flew south for five minutes, then started communication with the scout on the ground.

"Scout One, this is Banana Three, over."

"Scout One."

"Are you ready for extraction?"

"Roger. I'm inflating the balloon."

A large red balloon appeared at the edge of the jungle. It rose into the air, trailing a rope behind.

Banana Three slowed and dropped a hook from the open door.

Small arms fire broke out from the jungle. Bullets whizzed all around the chopper, some making hits.

The balloon rose to the chopper's height and the Green Giant swooped down to catch the rope with its hook. The chopper flew on and jerked a man off the ground.

Bullets continued to whiz by.

The chopper rose several thousand feet and reeled in the rope. Two crew members helped the man dressed in Vietnamese peasant attire onto the bird.

"Four Eyes, you son of a bitch," Gino yelled. He grabbed the little man and hugged him. "What the hell were you doing down there?"

"Keeping your asses safe."

The chopper headed home.

6

MISSION TO HANOI — NA TRANG SOUTH VIETNAM

SEPTEMBER 1969

G ino knocked on the office door.

"C'mon in, Top," Ordered Lieutenant Colonel Thompson, who wore his silver-hair high and tight.

Something was up. Activity buzzed around the camp for days.

"I need volunteers." The colonel grinned, sitting behind a worn metal desk. "Your A-team just volunteered."

"Sir, yes sir." Gino snapped to attention and saluted.

"You're going on a special mission. You will not wear uniforms and you will not use American weapons. No orders will ever be written down and the U.S. government will disavow any knowledge of your activities if you're caught. You will not be caught." Thompson stopped to let that sink in. "Is that clear, Sergeant?"

"Yes, sir."

"Okay, relax, Pancho. Take a look at the map here." Colonel Thompson stood and walked to a giant map of North Vietnam on the wall.

"You will be inserted here, just south of the DMZ. South Vietnamese sympathizers will meet you there. They will escort you, using the Underground Railroad in reverse, to Hanoi.

Gino heard rumors of the Underground Railroad. South Vietnamese sympathizers used the route to lead downed U.S. airmen through the night to the southern border. It was well organized and efficient. Dozens of airmen slept in warm beds thanks to their Vietnamese friends.

"I see . . ."

"Here are your orders," Thompson handed Gino a sealed envelope. "Burn it after reading it. Under no conditions will you let it fall into the hands of the enemy." Thompson sucked in a deep breath. "You got that, soldier?"

"Yes, sir." *What the fuck are we going to do in Hanoi?*

"You will not tell anyone of these orders. Once you are airborne, you may give your men their orders."

Gino nodded.

"Collect your men and report to the armory. You'll draw Chinese and Soviet weapons. You will wear civilian clothes. Not one word of this is to be leaked to anyone outside your A-team." Thompson's face looked drawn, and he had a twitch next to his right eye.

He looks like a judge handing down a death sentence.

"Is that clear, Sergeant?"

"Yes, sir."

"Then dismissed."

Gino turned to walk to the door. Thompson stopped him.

"I don't make up these orders, Pancho. I just execute them. May God help you."

Gino didn't turn back, he just walked out the door.

THE HUEYS DROPPED into the LZ. Gino was out the door before the chopper hovered. They wouldn't touch down. His men shoved canvas duffles out the door, and Gino and Sergeant Mo Smith, the intelligence officer and his second in command, organized the duffles.

The two six-man teams formed up as the choppers climbed out.

"All accounted for, Pancho," Smith told Gino.

Mohammed Smith was a tall, thin black man with a severely receding hairline. His broad nose had been broken numerous times and his eyes bulged. He carried a Soviet made IZh-58 double-barreled shotgun.

"Okay, ladies. Saddle up. We got ground to cover." Gino grabbed his pack and slung it across his shoulders. Then he picked up one of the duffles. It must have weighed fifty pounds.

The other eleven men, dressed in plantation owners' outfits, all made in Malaysia, picked through the pile and found their baggage.

"Move out." Gino took a deep breath. This was the beginning of what? *"Adelante, amigos."* His men fell in. "Gunnar, you take point. Carlson, drag." All of the A-team were sergeants.

Gunnar was a huge man of Norwegian heritage. His bright-red hair and beard as well as his size set him apart from the others. He had grown up in the Ballard section of Seattle where big Norsemen were the rule rather than the exception.

The men disappeared into the jungle.

Gino referred to his map. His Forward Air Coordinator was a small wiry Frenchman. He knew the location of the rendezvous. The guide did not know the insertion point. That way, if captured, he couldn't tell the enemy where the Green Berets were coming from.

"We should meet up with our guide in about five klicks. Keep your eyes peeled."

The jungle was hot and humid. Their clothes stuck to their bodies. The men frequently sipped from their canteens as they walked.

Animal sounds filled the forest from monkeys' cries to bird calls to the occasional elephant's trumpet. Gino heard running water, the jungle was anything but silent. The air smelled sweet and putrid.

Vines with bright flowers draped the trees. "Don't touch the flowers," Sergeant Smith said. "Some o'dem are deadly."

Gunnar led the troop along animal trails, always moving toward the north.

"Holy shit," Benson cried out.

A large lizard, at least five feet long, slithered across the path. Benson jumped back and the other men laughed.

"Just a monitor lizard, Benny," Jimenez said. "They won't eat you, you're too tough."

The march continued.

Gino referred to his map and compass frequently. His French FAC said hardly a word.

Smith came up from behind and smacked Gino on the ass. "We should be gettin' close, Taco Man."

"Can't be far. Maybe half a klick." Gino reached for his canteen. "We're meetin' them alongside the stream."

"Think we betta stop and take cover 'fore anyone moves into da open?"

"Roger that," Gino said.

Within fifteen minutes Gunnar raised his fist and the column stopped. He came hustling back to Gino.

"Small river up ahead. Waterfall, maybe twenty feet tall. Clearing around the fall."

"That sounds about right." Gino pulled out his map. "Okay, ladies, take cover. We'll sit and watch for a while."

The men faded into the forest, their clothes blending with the bushes.

"*Mes Amis*, I will leave you now," the FAC said. "My job is done." He faded into the jungle.

Gino and Smith found a large rock overlooking the scene. Gino pulled out his binoculars. "All quiet now."

"Le's jus' be cool, man," Smith said.

In about half an hour, two old Vietnamese men cautiously entered the clearing. They looked all around. Apparently, they saw nothing to worry them. They squatted down by the river.

Gino held up his hand. There was no movement or sound from his men.

After ten minutes of silence. Gino rose and started toward the clearing. "Cover me," he said to Smith.

Smith just snorted. "Like I'm gonna take a li'l nap right 'bout now?"

The Vietnamese men rose and walked toward Gino.

"Welcome," the bent man said. He had a long gray pointed beard and bushy eyebrows. "I am Han." He waved toward the other old man, also gray but not quite as bent. "This Duc."

"Gino." Gino held out his hand. "I hear the weather is bad up north." That was the pass code.

"Not as bad as one might think," Han said. The phrase checked out. "Better move. Need to find cover for rest of day. We go on after dark."

The old men led them away from the river to a hilly region covered by boulders. He found a cave that had obviously been used before.

"We stay here few hours."

AT DARK, the group set out again. The old Vietnamese men kept up a brutal pace. They moved through the dark like big cats.

They've spent their whole lives here. They probably know every rock and tree.

The Green Berets prided themselves on their toughness, but all of them gasped for breath like hooked fish when Duc called the first halt.

"We rest here. Ten minutes. Then we run across open land. Two kilometers."

Gino and Smith moved to the edge of the clearing. It was about two klicks wide and twice as long. The stream meandered through the open land.

"Hell of a sprint," Smith said.

"I don't smell any NVA." Gino insisted he had a sixth sense that let him smell the enemy.

"You willin' to bet your life, our lives, on that, Pancho?"

Gino dropped to one knee and touched the soil. "We don't got much choice. These old guys say this is the way."

At exactly the ten-minute mark, Duc rose and started across the field. Gino and his A-team followed fifty yards behind.

Gino held his breath while he started. That only lasted a few steps before he blew out a long breath and took in fresh air. The men's equipment rattled as they ran. Other than that, the clearing was silent.

Every moment Gino expected gunfire. He was prepared to throw himself to the ground.

The shots never came.

When Duc reached the river, he slowed. He stopped and studied the water while the rest of the troop caught up.

"I think safe. No see crocodiles."

Holy crap. That's all we need. We get by the NVA and get eaten by crocs.

The old men entered the water. They took slow, steady steps toward the other side holding their rifles over their heads. Gino's men imitated their movement.

All crossed without incident.

Duc ran for the jungle.

Safely inside the dense green cover, he stopped again to rest.

"God damn," Smith said. "How do those old guys keep it up? My grandpa would've died somewhere back in the jungle by now."

"These are tough country people," Gino said. "I'm just glad they're on our side."

About half an hour into their march, Gunnar raised his fist. He twisted his head to listen.

Gino hustled up to him to see what the problem was.

"What's up?" Gino saw no evidence of enemy troops.

"I heard something, Paco." He pointed toward the bushes lining their path.

Gino didn't see anything but darkness.

"There. There," Gunnar insisted.

"Jesus." Gino turned on his flashlight. A huge snake froze in the beam of light. It was dark with brown markings looking kind of like a road map, across its broad body. "Whadda ya think? Maybe ten feet."

Gunnar took a step back. "Na, bigger than that. This momma must be at least fifteen feet."

"Why you stop?" Duc came running back from his position in the lead.

"Snake." Gino pointed his flashlight. The snake's eyes reflected red in the bright light. It looked positively evil.

"No problem. Snake no bother you. Leave it alone and let's go. Turn off light. Don't want let anyone know we here."

And they were off again.

As dawn broke, they approached a tiny hamlet. Thatched roof hooches surrounded a central open area. Gino spotted a well and fire pit in the opening.

"Come with me," Duc said, and circled the hamlet. "We spend day here." He led them to an underground bunker covered in sandbags. "You can get out back way," he pointed to a ladder at the rear of the bunker, "if Army come."

The team settled in for the day. Vietnamese women brought them rice with tiny bits of fish in it and filled their canteens. None of them spoke English, but all were hospitable.

Soon the men slept.

7

THE FINAL ACT — HANOI

It took two weeks to travel approximately 400 miles from the DMZ to Hanoi. At each stop, the Underground Railroad conductors changed. No one conductor knew more than the stop before him and the stop after him. They were all old men. The Army grabbed all the young men.

The closer they got to Hanoi, the more the earth was decimated by bomb craters. Dikes around rice paddies were flattened. Whole forests were uprooted and burned. Only the dead could live here. And the Vietnamese.

Gino was beyond tired when they stopped at a small farm just outside Hanoi. He could see the tall buildings from the front stoop.

"Stand down, men." He sipped the last water from his canteen. "We're gonna stay here overnight."

He found a shady spot under a tree and Smith sat down next to him.

"It's time, huh?"

Gino nodded. "Yeah. I guess we better tell the boys what this is all about."

He whispered to Smith.

"Oh, God, no way, man." Smith shook his head. "That's crazy. That's impossible."

Gino held his face in his hands. "I don't know if I can do this."

"We gotta, man, or else we might as well join the commies. If we come home empty handed, there's gonna be hell to pay."

"But he's just an old man. How much can he have to do with the war anymore?"

"He's a symbol man, what woulda happened to the Union if the Rebs had knocked off Abe Lincoln?"

HIS ORDERS TOLD Gino to meet a Russian KGB double agent in Hanoi to get further instructions. He moved under the cover of night and found the skanky bar in the old section of town.

As Gino's eyes acclimated to the dimly lit bar, it became instantly apparent who his contact was. A large bear of a man sat with his back to a wall at a rickety table. He was the only other occidental in the bar.

Gino walked up to his table. "What is the Bolshoi performing this fall?"

The big Russian looked up at him. "Spartacus, of course." Spartacus was the Bolshoi's signature performance. "*Priveyet*, my friend." He waved his hand in a gracious gesture, signaling Gino to sit down.

"Dimitri," he said, extending his hand.

Damn, I might as well be wearing a neon sign saying, "SPY." Gino gulped and took the Russian's hand. "Paco."

"Mr. Paco, I hear you have a dangerous assignment."

No shit. "You're supposed to give us intel on where it's to take place."

Dimitri knocked back his shot of vodka and poured another glass for himself and one for Gino. "The target is giving a speech two days from now. He will speak from the walls of the

Imperial Citadel of Thang Long. There you will have your shot."

"What about guards?"

"It will be the best guarded place in Asia. You will have to determine how and where to deploy your men."

Dimitri pulled a manila envelope from his inner coat pocket and handed it to Gino. "Here are a map and floor plan of the palace. Don't open it here. Only open it when you are sure you're alone."

"How will we get past the guards?" Gino asked.

Dimitri held up both hands, palms out. "Not my problem." He finished his last shot of vodka and walked out.

"OKAY," Gino said as he spread the map on the floor for his team to see. "We need to leave troops here, here, here, and here. They'll cover our escape. Mo, you and Tsuko take the anchor position. I want to make sure we have a clear way out."

"Roger that," Smith said.

The A-team crowded into a little house on a street of little houses. The road was narrow and filled with bikes, scooters, and motor bikes spewing blue smoke. Trash was strewn liberally along the road. Everywhere the sounds of the metropolis included people yelling and talking, police sirens blasting, the clank of trollies in the distance.

The city reeked of sewage and rot. On the way in, Gino noticed bombed out sections. Whole blocks had been obliterated, some still smoking. He could smell death all around him.

Hanoi in war time.

"Gunnar, me and you will find a covered spot on the roof of this building."

"Ya, sure, you betcha," the red headed giant said. He was the best marksman in the team. Maybe the best marksman in the

Army. "Dis Russian rifle you got me is great. They claim ninety percent accuracy at two hundred yards." He lifted the Dragunov rifle for all to see.

"Well, it better be accurate at more than that. This won't be an easy shot." Gino turned to the other Mexican on the team. "Jimenez, you, Hardy, Washington, and Culpepper will cover the exit here. Once Gunnar takes the shot, we need to get out pronto."

They spent the day going over the plan, checking their equipment, cleaning their guns, and resting. Two young Vietnamese girls brought them rice and water.

AT 02:00 they left the safe house. The men split up; smaller groups were less likely to gather attention. As each group went to their assigned locations. Gino's team climbed in the back of a canvas covered truck. They made no sounds. Gino gave orders with hand signals. All the men darkened their faces to not be noticeable in the dark. They wore all-black clothes.

When they reached their target, Jimenez and his men slid out of the truck and melted into the night, finding positions from which to guard the entrance. If any police should show up, they would be hopelessly outgunned.

Gino and Gunnar ascended the staircase five floors to the roof. The door to the roof was padlocked. Gunnar had learned to defeat any type of Vietnamese padlock during training.

He wrapped a small metal shim around the fixed shackle. He applied pressure and pushed the point of the shim down the hole around the shackle. He did the same with the opening side of the shackle. With a faint click, the lock opened.

Still without a word, the two men made their way onto the roof. The wooden stairs creaked too loudly for Gino's liking. The building smelled musty, and Gino could almost feel the mold in the air. It was an old building. Over the decades the roof accumulated piles of refuse of one sort or another. Gunnar found a position where he had a clear shot at the lectern.

Gino and Gunnar moved piles of trash to cover their position. By daylight they were settled in.

"When you was growing up in Mexico, did you ever think you'd be doing anything like this?" Gunnar asked.

"Hell, when I was growin' up, all I could think about was how much I hated picking tomatoes, and baseball. If you'da me I'd be here now, I wouldn't a believed you."

Gunnar shook his massive red head. "Ya, me too. I thought I'd work on my father's fishing boat and take it over when he got too old to fish." He wiped his nose with the back of his hand. "I never thought I'd even be in the Army."

"How'd you get here?"

"Uncle Sam drafted me."

The men sat and waited hours for the festivities to begin. The early September sun beat down on their hideout.

The Imperial Citadel in Than Long covered blocks. The city grew up around it.

Five arched entrances covered the tall, gray, stone wall at the front of the complex. Then the wall turned into yellow stone. In the center of the complex a huge pagoda with a red roof with upturned spikes at each corner dominated the complex. Manicured trees carefully planted along the font of the wall complemented the lawn that stretched out for acres. Hundreds of thousands of people could congregate in front of the wall. Two wide sidewalks cut through the lawn to the outside arches in the wall. The center sidewalk that led to the central three arches was immense. *Jesus shit. That thing's wide enough to land a 747.*

A grandstand and platform were erected on top of the gray wall in the center. *That's gotta be where the speaker will stand.*

By mid-morning, people began to arrive. Crowds of civilians poured into the area carrying lawn chairs and coolers. Some just squatted on their haunches and ate from wicker baskets.

Little by little, the grandstand filled. By eleven-thirty, the stand was at capacity and the lawn area overflowed.

Gino sensed the excitement in the crowd. He wondered if Nixon gave a speech back home if anyone would care. There was electricity in the air.

At noon a group of policemen appeared on the platform, surrounding an old man in peasant attire.

He was a small, thin man with a long gray beard. He shuffled to the lectern with help from two men in Western business suits.

The crowd went wild. Everyone in the grandstand stood and applauded. The people below threw confetti in the air. The cheering went on for minutes.

Finally, the old man raised both hands and the crowd quieted.

JIMENEZ WAS the first to notice. A squad of NVA soldiers in full battle dress marched down the road.

"Heads up, guys, a gook squad coming."

The other three men readied their weapons. There was no way the NVA would get past them.

At the same moment six armed NVA stealthily approached Smith's position.

"Look out, Mo, we got company." Seargent Tsuko raised his AK-47 assault rifle.

"Shit, someone musta talked," Jimenez said, cocking his rifle.

The NVA squad opened fire. Jimenez and his men returned it.

They were ensconced in deep doorways or behind concrete barriers. The enemy fire did little damage.

Jimenez returned fire. Two NVAs went down.

The leader of the NVA squad signaled his men to take cover, then called up a man with a rocket launcher.

After a few words, the rocket man fired on a concrete barrier hiding two of Jimenez's men. The barrier exploded, sending deadly shrapnel in every direction. Two men were down.

"Get that bastard," Jimenez shouted.

Culpeper laid down fire and Jimenez took his time lining up the shot. Before Rocket man could fire again, three red spots appeared on his chest as he was flung backward.

The rest of the NVA squad fired away. Culpeper took a hit to the shoulder but kept fighting. You can't take out a Green Beret with a wound like that.

Then Jimenez took a gut shot. He collapsed to the ground.

"Jimmy, you okay?" Culpepper asked.

He never heard the answer. An NVA bullet hit him in the forehead.

SMITH AND TSUKO didn't have any better luck. They were out manned and out gunned. The Vietnamese soldiers were ready for them.

"Shit, they knew we were here," Tsuko said.

"I hope the others're doing better." Smith fired a burst at the enemy.

After a few minutes of fighting, both Smith and Tsuko went down.

The other teams fared no better. There were squads of NVA at each hideout location, waiting for them.

None of the groups could hold off the overwhelming number of enemy soldiers.

GINO HEARD the gunfire below him. "Take your shot," he yelled at Gunnar.

The door to the staircase crashed open and a group of NVA soldiers burst onto the roof. Gino took two of them out before they could find cover.

The trash pile Gino and Gunnar built to hide themselves was not bullet proof. North Vietnamese bullets easily penetrated. The only benefit the trash provided was that the enemy couldn't see them.

"Take the God damned shot." Gino returned fire. He glanced around at Gunnar to see him take a bullet in the back.

Gunnar yelled and lurched forward, dropping his rifle.

"Gunnar." Gino looked back at him, then turned to concentrate on the soldiers on the roof. "You hit bad man?"

Gunnar groaned and clawed himself back up into position. Blood poured from the hole in his back "Ya, I hit bad."

Gunnar picked up the sniper rifle and set it on the roof ledge. He put his eye to the scope. Bullets whizzed around him. He felt another impact in his thigh.

"Take the fuckin' shot," Gino screamed.

Gunnar couldn't hold the rifle still. The barrel swayed, the old man moved in and out of the crosshairs. A bullet hit the concrete ledge next to Gunnar and sent up a shower of shards.

Gunner took a deep breath. Put the cross hairs on the old man. His guards hadn't had time to react yet. One guard lurched toward the man.

Gunnar slowly squeezed the trigger.

The old man's head exploded. It was the last thing that Gunnar saw.

Gino continued to fire at the enemy soldiers. *I gotta get us outta here.* He looked around for a way out. He saw none. *God damn, what happened to Jimenez? He was supposed to cover our exit.*

The gunfire in the streets stopped. More NVA soldiers and policemen converged on the building.

Gino's magazine was empty. He dropped it out and reached for another.

The bullet caught him in the upper chest. His gun went flying one direction, the magazine the other.

He lay on the floor, blood oozing from his chest.

Mama, Papa. I love you.

He reached for the Soviet revolver in his belt. Another shot hit him in the shoulder and his arm went numb. A North Vietnamese soldier kicked him in the head. Everything went black.

BOOK II

CHUN

8

ESCAPE FROM VIETNAM - DA NANG AIRBASE

The government drafted Nguyen Van Chun two years ago, before he finished school. After basic training, his cousin, Lanh, and he were sent to flight school together. Chun mastered the giant C-130 cargo planes and Lanh became a flight engineer.

They made hundreds of trips to Hawaii and the Philippines, ferrying out the wounded and bringing in supplies. *All the guns, Jeeps, tanks, anti-aircraft guns, and all the spare parts in the world could not win this war,* Chun thought. The Americans pulled out their combat troops and the South Vietnamese Army was not up to the task of holding back the invaders.

The country collapsed.

Chun had no faith in his Army or his country. The leaders were riddled with corruption. The officers were incompetent. His primary mission was staying alive.

He knew the South Vietnamese soldiers were scared, poorly trained, and had no confidence in their leaders. Many simply refused to follow orders.

The North Vietnamese, on the other hand, had the latest Soviet weapons, were well trained, and loyal to their officers.

They moved and operated as one huge entity. They were moving south faster than Patton's march to Bastogne.

Chun knew it was over when rich South Vietnamese businessmen and government officials started showing up at the Da Nang airbase with families and trucks full of treasure in tow.

That started the nightmare. He and Lanh flew the first load, treasures included, to Con Lua Island off the Vietnamese coast. From there the passengers would take chartered airlines to the United States.

This went on for days. When senior officers and their families started showing up, Chun became concerned. How were he and Lanh going to get out of Vietnam? If the NVA captured them, only horror awaited.

The war scattered their families who knew where. He hadn't made contact with his parents in months.

"The generals are all gone," Lanh said. "When colonels start showing up, we're in real trouble."

The colonels and their families started loading onto Chun's plane later that day.

They had been flying for thirty-six hours straight, stopping only to refuel the giant plane. Chun and Lanh kept up a constant chatter to keep themselves awake.

When Lanh stopped answering him, Chun looked over and saw his cousin asleep in the co-pilot's seat. *Let him sleep. I'll need him when we get to Da Nang.*

Chun felt his forehead contact the steering yoke and sat up straight. "Oh, God. I almost fell asleep." The autopilot held them on course, but there needed to be a human at the controls to make split-second decisions.

The Army may have collapsed, but the Air Force held the line. South Vietnamese F-4 Phantom jets kept the North Vietnamese MIGs off the cargo planes. Even so, Chun expected every flight to be their last.

The April sky was clear and blue. How could anybody be unhappy on a day like this? But millions of South Vietnamese were unhappy. Scared. Apprehensive. As Chun and Lanh ferried rich, spoiled Vietnamese and American ex-pats out to Con Lua Island, while the masses hunkered down and waited for the invasion.

He piloted the big plane back to Con Lua. Sweat muddied his vision. His heart ran wild. Cold fingers ran up and down his spine.

He didn't see any Vietnamese Air Force cover.

They made it to the island. Neither Chun nor Lanh could keep their eyes open.

As Chun brought his plane onto final for the airfield on Con Lua, he saw massive piles of precious objects lining the runway. The evacuees brought as many valuables as they could carry but had to discard them so they could get a place on a plane to the U.S.

Chun brought the big plane down and the tires kissed the runway. He hit the brakes and reversed the thrust on the engines. The big gas-turbine engines whined, and the plane slowed down.

"Romeo Sierra Alpha Bravo one seven five," the tower said, "exit the runway and contact ground control on one oh one point seven."

Ground control directed Chun to a distant hangar where Air Force personnel waited. While the plane was still being unloaded, a fuel truck rushed to the scene and men began the refueling process.

Chun and Lanh had time to exit the plane, use the facilities, and grab a sandwich from the galley in the hangar. Then they were back in the plane being cleared to taxi to the runway.

The flight back to Da Nang was uneventful.

"Da Nang, this is Romeo Sierra Alpha Bravo one seven five. Landing."

There was no response.

Chun repeated the message three times and turned to Lanh. "There's nobody there."

"We have to land," Lanh said. "We pick up refugees."

They got the plane down and a contingent of South Vietnamese soldiers imposed some semblance of order. The soldiers allowed passengers to board. Luggage was thrown to the side of the runway.

The capacity of the C-130 Hercules was ninety-two passengers. These were seated on aluminum benches running fore and aft along the cabin sides. The plane was designed for military airlift, so the center of the cargo hold was built to carry Jeeps, tanks, and other weapons of war. On this trip, Chun counted more than two hundred people on his plane. They were crowded into the cargo area like sheep to slaughter.

The plane was sluggish as it clawed its way into the air. Chun used much more of the runway than he had ever done before. In the air, the plane handled like a pig.

When they landed on Con Lua, the ground crew told them they were finished. That was the last flight.

Until the next one.

"Nguyen, you're going back," a South Vietnamese captain told him. "We have reports of many women and children waiting at the air base for evacuation. We must make at least one more trip to get them out."

"Yes, sir." Chun's heart dropped to the bottom of his stomach. How much longer could the battered air base hold out? This was a suicide mission.

Nonetheless, they lifted his tired C-130 into the air and headed back to Da Nang.

He didn't bother calling approach control as they descended toward the airfield. He knew no one was in the tower.

"Look," Lanh pointed out the window. "There's nobody there. The base is deserted."

"Good, then we can turn around and get out of here."

As the plane touched down on the tarmac, hundreds of people suddenly appeared from behind the buildings. Men, women, children. Soldiers in uniform. Then came the Jeeps, trucks, scooters, and motor bikes. All in a mad dash to get on the airplane before anyone else could.

Chun felt the dampness in his arm pits, and his wet shirt clung to his back. *My God, what have we done to our country?*

Any pretense of order quickly disappeared. Armed soldiers pushed women and children aside to get on the plane. In several places, soldiers got in fights about who was going to get on and gunfire erupted.

"Go, go, go," Lanh shouted waving his arms. "We can't take any more."

Chun looked over his shoulder at the mass of humanity crawling through the cargo hold.

"Hang on." He advanced the throttles, and the big plane began to move down the runway.

Gunshots rang out. "They're shooting at us," Lanh yelled.

The Jeeps and trucks raced the plane down the runway. As they got in front of the plane they slowed down, trying to force the plane to stop.

Chun stomped on the left rudder pedal and the plane veered left. They bounced over the grass and bumped onto the taxiway. Chun gave the engines full throttle.

His move startled the Jeep and truck drivers. It took them several seconds to realize what happened and change their course toward the plane.

They were too late. The heavily loaded Hercules limped into the air.

"Chun, we got a problem," Lanh shouted into his headset. "The rear ramp won't close."

Chun looked back over his shoulder. Dozens of men, women and children clung to the ramp as the plane gained altitude. One by one, people fell from the ramp. Chun was at two thousand feet. There was no hope for those that fell off.

"Get them aboard," Chun yelled. "Get some of the soldiers to help you."

The terrified soldiers wouldn't move toward the ramp for fear they would be thrown off.

Lanh strapped on a safety belt and inched closer to the ramp.

He held out his hand. "Come on. Give me your hand." A tiny woman grabbed on. Lanh pulled her to safety.

More people fell from the ramp. They couldn't move up the ramp due to the hurricane force wind generated by the plane's speed.

"Here, come to me," Lanh shouted.

Another soldier fell to his death. The plane climbed past five thousand feet.

One by one, the people on the ramp lost their grip and fell. The last to go was a woman. She desperately called out to Lanh.

"Take my baby." She extended her baby toward him.

He tried to reach the baby. Too far. He watched in horror. After what seemed an eternity, Lanh unhooked his safety belt and inched his way down the ramp. He grabbed the baby and crawled back to the safety of the plane. He turned to rescue the woman, but she was gone. Lanh looked, on terrified as she fell. She looked up at Lanh, mouthed "thank you," and waved goodbye.

Lanh stared at the stream of falling people. He couldn't believe what he was seeing.

He turned away and lifted the ramp. Tears flowed down his cheeks. Then he noticed the tall American with a camera on his shoulder.

"No," Lanh shouted and charged the man.

The big American took his charge and fell into the crowd of Vietnamese soldiers.

"I'll kill you." Lanh looked around for a weapon.

Hands grabbed at him, holding him back.

Eventually he regained his calm.

He worked his way forward to the co-pilot's seat and collapsed, sobbing and holding his fists over his eyes.

Chun radioed ahead and told his superiors what happened. They had an armed guard of American troops waiting for the plane to land.

The South Vietnamese soldiers were arrested as they

deplaned. An officer grabbed the American with his camera and led him off.

Walter Cronkite would play the video on CBS News that night.

"YOU MUST GO BACK," the lieutenant colonel said as he paced his office. "There are still women and children there that need to be evacuated."

"No. It's suicide. There are armed soldiers who'll kill to get on. They shot at us to keep us from taking off. It's a 'If I can't go, then no one else can go,' attitude."

The colonel put his hand on Chun's shoulder. "I know. You are the last plane we have left. We can't leave those people there to be murdered by the communists."

"On our last flight, we saw communist tanks moving south. What if they get there before we do?"

The colonel shook his head. "That's why you have to leave now. You can't waste a minute."

"But we have to refuel the plane."

"You don't have time. You can refuel in Da Nang before you come back."

Chun knew what waited for them at the end of the flight. The Communists would torture Lanh and him. They would put them in re-education camps to brainwash them. If they survived. With the base in danger of falling, the fighter jets that had kept the airspace clear for them had surely fled. They might get shot down before they even got there.

He also knew that to refuse an order, especially in those panicked times, meant death. They had to go.

FROM THE AIR, everything looked peaceful and serene. Da Nang Airbase sat at the end of Da Nang Bay, surrounded by tall mountains. Two parallel runways and the taxiways were the first thing Chun saw as they approached.

They made a pass over the base at two thousand feet. There was no movement. The hundreds of various kinds of aircraft were all gone. It looked like a ghost town.

Chun brought his bird around and entered the landing pattern. He and Lanh went through the landing checklist.

At the touch of a button, the flaps came down and the plane's nose pitched upward. Chun trimmed the plane to level attitude. He dropped to twelve hundred feet as he entered the downwind leg.

At eight hundred feet, he turned ninety degrees to the cross-wind leg. Still no movement below.

"Chun, look," Lanh cried out. He pointed out the window to the north.

Chun saw a column of North Vietnamese tanks threading their way through Hai Vanh pass. They were ugly things. Painted olive drab, with sloping armor to deflect shells. The long gun protruded over a complex, single piece of forward armor. Their treads moving through the mud with fearful efficiency.

"Christ. We got to land. We don't have any fuel." Sweat poured down Chun's face.

"Then let's get in and out quick. I don't care if we pick up any women or not." Lanh couldn't take his eyes off the tanks.

At six hundred feet, Chun turned up wind and lined up on the runway. Still not a word from the tower.

The big plane's wheels touched down with a screech as rubber met concrete. Chun stood on the brakes and reversed thrust. The plane slowed.

"Where do we go?" Chun asked.

"Try to find a maintenance hangar." Lanh wiped his brow. "There should be fuel there."

Chun taxied off the runway and headed to the maintenance bay.

The fuel trucks were all gone. The drivers must have used them to flee.

Chun taxied past the first hangar. Nothing there.

"Look." Lanh pointed as they came opposite the second hangar. "Fuel drums."

Chun stopped and secured the plane.

Lanh dropped the cargo door and they walked out into the silence of defeat. Not a soul was visible. Not even any dogs or other animals. The base sat there as if awaiting its death at the hands of the NVA.

"We got to lift those barrels on top of the wing," Chun said.

"But how?" The fifty-five-gallon fuel drums weighed about three hundred fifty pounds each. Chun and Lanh were not big men.

They scoured the area in search of something that could help.

"Chun, I found it," Lanh shouted.

He steered a four wheeled cherry-picker toward the stack of barrels.

He and Chun managed to wrestle a fuel drum onto the cherry picker. They drove it to the plane and hit the up button. The contraption shook. It felt like it would roll over and die. Then it started to go up. Slowly, the oil barrel rose to within two or three feet of the wing top.

Chun jumped on the wing. "You push, I'll pull."

Their fear surged as the two men attempted to raise the oil barrel to the wing.

"Lanh, look." Chun pointed to the north.

The column of North Vietnamese tanks crested the pass and headed down into the valley. Within a few minutes, Chun and the plane would be in range of their cannon.

With a grunt, Lanh gave a great shove. Chun pulled for all he was worth. The adrenaline kicked in. They managed to heave the heavy barrel onto the wing.

71

Chun fit the pump to the hole on the top of the drum. Lanh opened the filler hole. When Lanh put the hose from the pump into the hole, Chun started pumping.

Up and down. Up and down. Chun lost track of the number of times he pumped at somewhere around one hundred strokes. His arm ached. His breath came fast. And still he pumped.

The first shell fell well short of their position. Concrete and steel flew into the air on the taxiway several hundred meters from them.

The explosion motivated Chun and Lanh even more.

They finished the first barrel, rolled it off the wing, and went for another. This time, they had less trouble lifting the drum onto the wing.

Lanh took his turn pumping. With each volley, shells fell inexorably closer to the plane.

"Let's go get another,' Lanh said.

Then a shell fell close enough that Chun and Lanh were covered with dirt, rocks, and various debris. Their ears rang and their lungs filled with dust.

"To hell with it." Chun coughed. "Let's go."

"But Chun, we don't have enough fuel."

Chun slithered down from the wing top. "I'd rather take my chances with sharks than with those tanks."

Both men dashed to the rear of the plane and up the cargo door. Lanh closed the door as Chun made for the cockpit.

The engines roared with fresh fuel aboard. Lanh slid into the co-pilot's seat as Chun taxied toward the runway.

A shell fell exactly where the plane sat seconds ago. Debris rained down on the plane's aluminum skin and pinged like hail on a tin roof.

Chun left the taxiway and rumbled across the grass strips zigging and zagging to avoid a predictable path to the runway. Shells continued raining down.

They made it to the runway and Chun swung the big bird into the wind. He thrust all four throttles forward and the plane lurched under the almost twenty-thousand horsepower of its four engines.

Shells fell on the runway. Huge holes appeared all around them. Chun deftly maneuvered the clumsy plane around the holes as they reached take-off speed. Then they were in the air.

BOOK III

TED

PRESENT DAY

9

A MYSTERY REVEALED — SEATTLE

T ed Higuera's lungs felt heavy and damp from the hot, moist jungle air. Sweat drenched him as he walked through the dense foliage. But to where?

Why am I here? Where is here?

Night sounds filled the jungle. Birds calling, monkeys chattering, and an occasional roar far away. A fetid odor filled the air.

A glimmer of light peeked through the canopy. Ted looked up and saw a full moon through occasional breaks in the jungle roof. Little pools of light gave Ted enough vision to make his way forward. It wasn't really a trail, more of an animal path through the heavy forest.

Blue light flickered ahead.

A blue fire?

Ted crept cautiously toward the flames.

The jungle gave way to a clearing, A large pile of yellow stones filled the open space. The stones were on fire.

That's impossible. Rocks can't burn.

The pile of stones, higher than Ted's head, burned with a blue flame. Slow rivers of flame dripped down the pile's side. The rivers were the consistency of molasses. Occasional pops shot drops of fire into the air like Roman candles. The stench of sulfur filled the clearing.

Ted turned to a noise behind him.

Two small, brown soldiers carrying large machetes, stood and watched him.

Ted held up his hands in a gesture of peace. "Hi, there. I mean you no harm. Where am I?"

The men looked at each other, spoke in an unintelligible tongue, and charged Ted.

Ted turned and ran. *I can outrun those little bastards.*

And out-run them he did. With the speed that made him an All-City running back in Los Angeles, he sped down the path. *They didn't call me Twinkle-Toes for nothing.*

Something caught his foot and he sprawled on his face. Quickly he pushed himself to his knees and turned. The little men with the big knives were upon him.

A mighty roar filled the jungle. A huge black jaguar flew toward the first man. Ted heard the bones in the man's neck crack as the big cat landed on him.

The other man turned to flee. He got three steps. The jaguar took two bounds and was upon him.

Ted got to his feet and backed away. There was no way he could outrun a jaguar, and he had no weapon.

So, this is how it ends.

The big cat turned to Ted and stood, panting. He looked Ted up and down. Slowly he walked toward Ted.

Ted's heart jumped to his throat, his breath so fast he couldn't hold a breath.

The cat stopped two feet from Ted and sniffed the air. After an eternity, the cat took another step and sniffed at Ted.

"Oscar?" *No, it can't be. Oscar died years ago.*

The cat leaned forward and rubbed his head against Ted's leg.

"Oscar?" It had to be. "You're the same cat that saved me in Teotihuacan, aren't you?" He stroked the cat's head.

"I never believed in Aztec mythology, but are you Tlaloc?"

The big jaguar disappeared in a flash of smoke.

The smoke from the burning rocks swelled in volume. From out of the smoke a figure emerged.

A wizened, old, dark-skinned woman took shape. Her gray braid reached to her waist, and she wore a peasant blouse and a long green and white skirt.

"Abuelita?" Ted's grandmother was long dead.

The woman's steps never touched the ground. She walked on air.

"Teddy, it is so good to see you," she said in Spanish.

"Abuelita. Why are you here? How?"

The old woman raised her hands to shoulder level, palms down. "He is alive, *mijo*. You must find him."

"Who? Who is alive?"

"Go to him. He needs you."

"Abuelita . . . "

Ted bolted up in his bed and wiped his forehead. He was covered in sweat. His heart beat a wild tattoo in his chest and a chill ran down his spine. The bedclothes were drenched in sweat.

"Who, Abuelita? Who is still alive?"

"GOOD EVENING, LADIES AND GENTLEMEN," the pilot said in a distinct southern accent. "We are beginning our approach to Seattle-Tacoma International Airport."

Kathy Nguyen couldn't sit still in her office, or a courtroom, much less a plane. Her energy level was so high, she had to be up and around. Constantly moving. Always doing something. It was her one major flaw as a defense attorney.

After countless trips to the restrooms and endless chats with the flight attendants, Kathy knew their names, where they were from, their siblings, parents, etc. *If this fucking flight would just end—*

She stood in the galley and fumbled with the metal tags in her jacket pocket. *Are these really that important? Do I turn them over to the Army, or do I check with Chris's friend Ted first? That's his last name, isn't it? Higuera? I seem to remember he mentioned that he had an uncle or something go MIA in Vietnam.*

She returned to her seat and fastened her seat belt. Seventeen hours in the air was beyond torture. Her father, Chun, sat next to her. He hardly moved since they took off from Hanoi. So calm. So still. She wanted to yell at him to get up, move around, get some air. He possessed the innate ability to nod off anywhere.

The big plane touched down and Kathy and Chun joined the long entry line. It took nearly a half-hour to clear customs. She knew her mother and her brother, Eugene, waited patiently to pick them up.

TWO WEEKS of nothing but Vietnamese food made Kathy grateful that her mom prepared mac and cheese for dinner.

After dinner, Kathy retired to her room and collapsed on the bed.

How do I tell him? Should I call? Or let Chris make the contact?. Even though Chris is Ted's best friend, he's still my boss.

She reached in her purse and retrieved a pair of stainless steel tags on a chain.

PEACE FILLED the Queen Anne neighborhood of Seattle as Ted pulled the Blue Bomber, a Range Rover modified to withstand an IED blast, to the curb. His partner, Catrina Flaherty, ordered the SUV from the same company that built presidential limousines.

He hopped out and walked to the door of Mama's house. He didn't knock, just walked in.

The four-bedroom house had a great view of Puget Sound. The terracotta-painted walls of the living room had a geometric pattern border that reminded Ted of Aztec temples.

The furniture was old but serviceable.

"*Buenos noches,* Mama," Ted greeted.

His mother, a tiny Mexican woman dressed in a bright red bathrobe, sat on the sofa watching an old movie on TV. She hopped up at Ted's entrance and turned off the TV. Barely coming to Ted's chin, she had deep brown eyes and black hair, her beauty still shining through.

"Eduardo, what are you doing here at this time of night?" She reached for him and gave him a big *abrasso.*

"I have to talk to you. Something happened. I had a dream."

"Not another dream." His sister, Hope, said as she entered the room wearing an oversized T-shirt and boxer shorts. "What was it about ... Maria?" Her tone was almost snotty.

Ted plopped down in an overstuffed chair. "No, this was different. Abuelita came to me."

"I better make some chocolate," Mama said and headed for the kitchen.

Hope leaned against the door frame. "Abuelita? Is that unusual? Do you dream about her often?"

"No. I don't think I ever dreamed of her before." Ted stopped and took a breath. "You don't remember her, do you? Abuelita came to live with us when you were a little girl."

"I remember when she died." Hope eased herself onto the sofa.

"There was always something almost mystical about her. She was a *curandera*, you know?"

"You mean she healed people?"

"Yeah, and a lot more. People came to her with their problems, and she told them how to fix 'em. People gave her a lot of respect."

"Here we are." Mama re-entered the living room with a tray that had a terracotta pot and three cups and saucers. There were also several pieces of *pan dulce* on a plate.

Mama took the lid off the pot and inserted a wooden instrument with a round base and loose rings around it. She rubbed the handle between her hands and beat the chocolate to a froth. She removed the *molinillo*, and poured the three cups of chocolate.

"Now, what were you saying about Abuelita?" she asked in accented English.

Ted took his cup and savored the sweet, spicy flavor. "Mama, I had a really weird dream. Abuelita came to me. She said that he wasn't dead. That I must find him. He needed me."

Hope leaned forward as she accepted a cup from Mama. "Who isn't dead?"

"That's just it. I don't know."

"Maybe Papa?" Hope asked.

"Not possible. We all saw Papa's body."

"And that's all. Just your grandmother coming to you." Mama took a piece of *pan dulce* from the plate.

"No, there was a lot of other stuff. I was in a jungle, and two men attacked me. Then a jaguar saved me."

Hope's eyes nearly popped. "Holy shit. A jaguar?" She looked down at her hands in her lap. "Isn't that the same thing that happened in Mexico?"

"Yeah. The big cat took out two cartel soldiers that were going to shoot me. I think it was Oscar. But he's been dead for years."

"Could Tlaloc still be looking after you?" Hope took Aztec mythology seriously. "I did some study after we got back. Tlaloc is a shape shifter, and he takes the form of a jaguar when he comes to Earth."

"I know it's crazy, but I'm sure the jaguar in Mexico was Oscar. When I got back from Mexico, Oscar had exactly the same wounds as the jaguar."

"I know we're pushing the boundaries of reality," Hope said, "but could Oscar really have changed into a jaguar? Could Tlaloc really have saved you?"

Mama gently put her cup in its saucer. "Maybe that's who she says isn't dead. Maybe she wants you to find Oscar."

Ted shook his head. "No. It can't be. Oscar was thirteen years old when he died. And that was what, five or six years ago. He couldn't possibly be alive." He reached for his cup. "Besides, I buried him. I know he was dead."

"What else. Was there anything else in your dream?" Hope asked.

"This is really weird. There was this big pile of yellow rocks that burned with a blue flame, and smelled like shit."

Mama shot Ted a nasty look. "Fire and brimstone. If you went to church with us you would know that Father Xavier talks about it all the time. That's what Hell is made of. Lakes of burning stones. Rivers of fire running down the hills."

"Jesus." Ted clamped his hand to his mouth. "Do you think it means the devil is involved?"

Hope crossed herself. "What else could it mean. Abuelita wants you to save someone from Satan."

"Holy Christ."

"What are you going to do?" Mama asked.

Ted sat silent for a long second. "I ... I don't know. What can I do? I don't know who I'm supposed to save."

BORED OUT OF HIS MIND, Ted leafed through *Cybersecurity* magazine for what must have been the fourth time. He had no security checks running and the current investigations were all handled by Mary Beth.

The phone rang. *Thank God. Maybe it's a new case.*

"Hello, Flaherty & Associates, Ted Higuera here." Ted didn't recognize the phone number.

"Hi, Ted. I'm Kathy Nguyen, a partner at Chris's law firm."

The voice was vaguely familiar. He dug deep into his memory. "Oh, yes... I remember... You worked on my brother's case."

"That's right. That was my first case at Hardwick and Hardwick."

The image of Carlito standing at the defendant's table, accused of murder, filled Ted's mind. "We can't thank you enough for setting him free."

"You're welcome, but that's not why I called."

Ted wrinkled his brow. "What can I do for you, Kathy?"

"It's what I can do for you." Kathy's voice sounded slightly breathless and hesitant.

"Oh?"

"I have something that I think belongs to you. Something I brought back from Vietnam."

"Vietnam?" *How could anything from that part of the world have anything to do with me?*

"Yes. I just got back from a trip to the old country with my father. I found something there that might interest you."

Ted scratched his head. "Okay. So, what is it?"

"I think we need to meet in person. This is something you have to see."

A Pioneer Square institution, Larry's Green Door was built back somewhere during the Klondike Gold Rush. Patrons' carvings covered the walls and ceilings. Inside of a heart: "Tom loves Mary." Under a stick figure with giant boobs: "For a good time call—"

It was easier to meet Kathy at a location near her Smith Tower office. Ted's job left him free to roam the city at his discretion. He sat at a wooden booth nursing a Corona until a tiny woman with dark eyes and shiny black hair entered the bar.

Kathy. *She looks just like she did during the trial.*

Barely five feet tall, her beige business suit emphasized her slender waist and hips. She had the power of the sun in her dark eyes. He estimated she was about five years older than his thirty-one years.

Ted rose and extended his hand. "Hi, Kathy."

"Good to see you again." She shook his hand firmly, smoothed the back of her skirt, and eased into the booth opposite Ted. "Chris mentions you from time to time, but I don't think I've seen you since Carlito's trial."

"It's been a while." Ted grinned. "You look great."

She paused for a moment and looked at Ted's face. "I don't mean to pry, but what happened to your face?"

Ted ran his hands over his cheeks, feeling each one of the little scars. "I was helping the DHS with a terrorist case. When we cornered them, they blew up their building. I was lucky— just got a bunch of shrapnel in my face. One of the agents I was with was killed, the other lost a leg."

"My God." Kathy put both hands on the table and leaned forward. "I'm so sorry."

"It is what it is. No more *telenovela* roles for me." He chuckled and took a sip of beer to give him time to think. "What have you been doing?"

"I just got back from a trip to Vietnam."

A waiter appeared and took her drink order. A Manhattan.

"So you said."

"My father wanted to see the old country again. We toured Hanoi and the cities for a while, then we went into the back country to look for his family."

"Sounds like a good trip."

"It was a harsh trip. We were way back in the bush. No toilets, no running water. We took a bus as far as we could go, then we hiked miles to his village. My dad found his father still alive. My grandfather lived in a thatched hut with no running water or toilet. No electricity or Internet; they were totally off the grid."

She pushed back her long black hair from her eyes. "My grandfather had been a conductor on the Underground Railroad during the war."

"Underground Railroad?" Ted raised his empty beer bottle for the waiter to see. "What's that?"

"During the war, many anti-communist sympathizers lived in the North. My dad told me stories about how his father helped downed U.S. fliers escape to safety."

"Okay." Ted waited for the waiter to serve Kathy the Manhattan and give him a new beer. "But what does all this have to do with me?"

Kathy lifted her glass to her lips and sipped. "Mmm ... good. We were sitting around the campfire one night and Grandpa Duc told us a story about sneaking a group of America soldiers *into* North Vietnam."

"I'm still with you." Ted's gut tightened and he leaned forward. "But still, what does this have to do with me?"

Kathy traced the circles on the tabletop left by numerous glasses with her index finger. "He had something one of the soldiers left with him." She paused, then reached in her pocket and passed Ted the dog tags.

"Dog tags?" He turned them over and his mouth dropped open "My God! These belonged to my uncle."

"I didn't know what to do with them. There must have been hundreds of GIs named Higuera. But I took the chance that you should see them."

Ted choked up and his eyes moistened. "My uncle died in Vietnam. I think it was 1969. How could your grandpa get these?" Ted stared at the dog tags in his open hand.

"He said that your uncle and his team were on a secret mission into the North. They left their dog tags with him so that they couldn't be identified if they were killed or captured."

"But how did you get Uncle Gino's?" Ted's hands shook.

"Grandpa said that he returned a pile of dog tags to an American pilot they were taking south. The pilot must have dropped your uncle's because Grandpa found them in their hideout weeks later."

Ted shook his head. "My God. Papa never knew what happened to Gino. He went MIA. This happened before I was born. I don't think Mama even knew Gino. Papa was just a kid when Gino joined the Army." He closed his eyes and took a deep breath. "My grandparents are all dead. I have to show this to Mama, but I don't think she knows how to contact any of Papa's siblings."

"There's more, Ted. My grandfather heard that there's still a POW camp deep in the Quang Binh Province somewhere north of the Song Gianh River. Some of the most inaccessible jungle in Vietnam and they're holding an American GI."

Ted almost spit out his beer. "POWs? After all these years? Why would they still be holding 'em?"

Kathy leaned across the table and said in a soft voice. "I have no idea, but I thought you'd want to know."

Ted nodded, unable to speak.

THE DECISION — SEATTLE

C hris Hardwick, Esq. got to *El Nuevo Chapparal* first. He found the large, round booth in the back of the bar empty. Hope hurried out to meet him. She was short, dark, and beautiful. Her long black hair hung in a braid that reached all the way to her bottom and her coal-black eyes sparkled when she saw him.

"Hmm ... Mr. Hardwick, what can we do for you today?"

"I don't think you want to do it in the bar."

She tossed him a million-watt smile. "Maybe I do."

He held back a grin. They had gotten engaged when Hope was in the hospital recovering from gunshot wounds she received in Mexico. *I came so close to losing her ...*

"Is Ted coming?" she asked. After her father was killed in Mexico, the family sold Papa's restaurant and moved to Seattle to be close to her older brother, Ted. She opened *El Nuevo Chapparal* with the money from Papa's restaurant.

"Yeah. And one of my partners, too. Kathy Nguyen."

"Rico," Hope called to a waiter. "A Dos Equis for my friend here and bring a plate of nachos."

The waiter nodded and punched the order into his handheld device.

Ted snuck up, lifted his sister off the ground, and twirled her around. "*Hermana.* How's my favorite sister?"

"Let me down." Hope slapped his hands. "I'll bet you say that to all your sisters."

Chris studied his friend. Ted had put on a little weight around the middle since his college football days. He was short, a full six inches shorter than Chris's six-foot two-inch frame, but powerfully built, with a barrel chest and broad shoulders.

Chris couldn't help but feel sorry when he looked at Ted's scarred face. *Oh, well, it's the man inside that counts.*

"Teddy, good to see you." He reached out for Ted's hand.

Ted slid into the booth next to him and gave him a bro hug.

"What's the big deal?" Chris asked. "You called this meeting on short notice."

Ted waved a finger at the bartender. "I got some important news. It came from Kathy, so I invited her to join us. I've been doing some research, too."

The Dragon Lady entered the bar. Chris had worked for her as a paralegal at his father's law firm. She worked harder and pushed her paralegals more than any attorney at the firm.

When he had a high-profile murder case at his own firm, she was the first one he called for help. It hadn't taken long to make her a full partner.

"Kathy. Thanks for coming." Ted rose slightly behind the table to welcome her.

Hope reached over and gave her a hug. "What's this all about, *Chiquita?*" she asked.

"I'll let Ted tell you."

The drinks came, followed closely by a huge platter of nachos.

"Okay, now that I've got your attention," Ted said, "Kathy brought something back from Vietnam." He tossed the dog tags onto the table.

Chris picked them up. "I know what these are." He held them

close to Hope so she could read them. "Augustin Higuera? Is he related?"

Ted sipped his beer. "He was my uncle. Went MIA in Vietnam in sixty-nine." Ted glanced at Kathy. "Kathy can fill in the story."

He caught Kathy with a nacho in her mouth. She covered her lips with a hand and chomped down a few times then swallowed. "Ted's uncle was lost on a mission to North Vietnam." She took a quick sip of her Margarita. "My grandfather helped smuggle him into Hanoi, then he was never heard from again. While I was on a trip to Vietnam with my father, we found my grandfather still alive. He gave me those dog tags. He hoped I could find Gino's family and give them to them."

Chris leaned forward, both elbows on the table.

"I suspected the soldier might be related to Ted, and I was right." She took another sip of her Margarita. "I also heard a rumor. It's totally unsubstantiated, but I heard there's still a POW camp, and they're holding an American GI."

Chris digested the information. "Why would they still be holding a POW after all these years?"

"I had a dream," Ted mumbled.

"What was it, Dr. King?" Chris asked.

Ted gave him a "humph" and continued. "My grandmother came to me and said that he was alive. That I had to help him."

Chris slowly shook his head. "Ted, it was only a dream. The odds are fantastic that it could be your uncle."

"But if there's a chance, I have to try."

The table went silent.

"But why would they still be holding him?" Chris asked.

"Maybe he knows something they don't want the world to know," Kathy said.

"In that case, they would just shoot him," Chris said.

"I guess he could have done something that really pissed them off and they didn't want to return him," Hope added. "Do you think Tio Gino could be that prisoner? Could he still be alive?"

"The chances are very slight that it's him." Chris shook his head. "It's highly unlikely that the story is true. The U.S. and Vietnamese governments have been cooperating, trying to locate MIAs for years now. They would have found something."

Ted swiped at condensation on his beer bottle with his thumb. "Not if it's so secret that the Vietnamese wouldn't want word to get out." He gulped. "What if that prisoner knows something so important that it would rock the world?"

"You've been reading too many Tom Clancy novels, *hermano*," Hope said.

"But if there's a chance— Ted's voice trailed off.

"What do you want to do, bro?" Chris already knew the answer. "Go traipsing around some of the deepest, densest jungles in the world?"

Chris caught the slight grin on Ted's face. *Oh my God. You're going to do it.*

"Kathy, do you think your boss could give you another couple of weeks of vacation?" Ted smiled at Chris.

Before she had a chance to answer, Hope spoke up. "This is totally insane. We don't have any proof. Even if the camp exists, we don't know where it is. *If* it exists, we don't know if the prisoner is Uncle Gino. Ted — "

Ted interrupted, "But if it is Uncle Gino, we have to try. We have to find out what happened to him."

"Who is this Uncle Gino anyway?" Chris asked.

"Papa's oldest brother." Ted set his beer on the table. "He snuck into the U.S. from Mexico, then got in some legal trouble. They gave him the choice to go to prison or join the Army. He was a Green Beret in Vietnam when he disappeared."

There was a moment of silence while the group digested the information.

"He's the reason Papa came to the States." Ted rolled his beer bottle between his hands.

"Papa was ten-years old when Tio Gino left for the U.S. When Gino disappeared, six-years later, Papa decided to come to the U.S. to find out what happened. He dragged Mama north and they got married in L.A. He spent the rest of his life searching for clues to Gino's whereabouts." He stared at the table. "I owe Papa this."

"And why do you think this supposedly imprisoned GI is your uncle?"

Ted stared into space. "I don't know. I just have this gut feeling. Abuelita told me he was still alive."

We've done some pretty crazy shit on Ted's gut feelings, but this? A trip around the world to look for a missing uncle? "When do we leave?" Chris asked.

"Not yet." Ted's fingers drummed the table. "I need to do some research, ask a couple of friends for help. I'll let you know."

"I'm going, too," Hope cut in. "You don't think I'm going to let my brother and my fiancé go stumbling around Vietnam looking for my uncle alone, do you? Somebody needs to hold the reins on you two."

Chris had been through this before. "There's no use fighting you. You always find a way to be included." *Besides, she's an asset.* A dead shot with a pistol and a genius at throwing knives, not to mention that she was smart as a whip and a consummate actress.

Ted turned to Kathy. "And you? Do you feel like playing Wonder Woman?"

Kathy was silent for almost a minute. "I need to think about it. I need to talk to my father. He has wisdom beyond compare."

TED GAZED at Mama at the kitchen table shucking peas. She worked quietly and efficiently. Occasionally she stopped for a drink of Diet 7-Up.

Mama had the mid-twentieth century kitchen remodeled when she moved in. The solid oak cabinets and stainless steel appliances sparkled with the twenty-first century. The table, however, was a throwback. Mama had owned it for most of her life. With a butcher-block top and white legs, it was perfect for rolling out tortillas or prepping a large feast.

"So what is it, *hijo?* You seem troubled."

Ted reached for a *buñuelo* from the plate on the table. "I know what Abuelita meant." He took a bite. "Mmm . . . they just keep getting better."

"Go on, Teddy." Mama waved away the compliment. "What did Abuelita mean?"

"Do you remember Uncle Gino? The brother Papa always talked about?"

"I never met him. But your father talked about him all the time."

Ted got up and went to the refrigerator. "What was he always saying about Gino?" He poured himself a glass of milk.

"What was he saying? I don't know." Mama looked up from her work. "What are you getting at, *Mijo?*"

"Don't you remember? Papa always talked about how Gino was lost in Vietnam. How he spent hours and hours calling, writing, talking to anyone who might know about MIAs."

"So?"

"A friend of mine just went to Vietnam to look for her grandfather. She brought these back with her." Ted handed the dog tags to Mama.

Her face wrinkled in curiosity. "What are these?" She turned them over in her hand. "*Ay, Dios Mio.*" She dropped them on the table. "These are Gino's." She crossed herself.

"She also said that she heard that there may be a prisoner of war camp still active. Do you think Gino could possibly be there?"

Mama dropped her peas and shook her head. "That's impossible. It's been such a long time. How could he possibly still be alive?"

"But, Mama, remember what Abuelita told me in my dream? He's alive. He needs my help. I have to find him."

Mama got up and walked to the sink. She leaned her hands on the stainless steel and gazed out the window.

Mama let out a deep sign and turned to him. "You're going after him, aren't you? I know you, just like your papa."

Ted got up and walked over to his mother. "If there's any chance that Gino's alive, I have to go." He took both of Mama's hands in his. "I owe it to Papa."

Mama lowered her head and gently shook it. "I suppose you're going to take your crazy sister with you, aren't you?"

"I couldn't get Hope to stay behind if I tried. She's her own person."

Tears welled in Mama's eyes. She turned away from Ted and wiped her face with the tail of her apron. "Be safe, *Mijo*. Go with God."

11

DANGER ON THE BEACH — BAI TU BAY, VIETNAM

hree battered Mercedes-Benz two-ton trucks bumped down the dirt road. They had left Laos more than six hours prior and took two ferries to reach Bai Tu Bay.

The bay was one of Vietnam's hidden treasures. As a UNESCO World Heritage site, only a limited number of tours and cruises were allowed on the bay. The villages around the bay missed the tourist rush and remained quiet fishing villages.

The dark green of the surrounding mountains contrasted with the turquoise waters of the inlet. Sheer cliffs fell hundreds of feet into the water. Rounded mounds of rock filled the bay close to shore.

Lying offshore, past the rocky mounds, a rusty old tramp steamer swung at anchor. The captain, dressed in a fisherman's sweater, khaki pants, and wearing a yachting cap that was once white, paced the bridge. "They're late," the Filipino captain growled.

The crew on the bridge deck, a United Nations of men, cowered and no one answered.

"Those sons-a-bitches better be here before the turn of the tide, or we leave without them."

A weary landing craft rafted up to the steamer. Three men waited aboard for the orders to run up onto the beach.

The trucks crested the mountains and continued down toward the wide, sandy beach. With huge traction tires, they had no problem negotiating the sand.

The passenger in the lead truck picked up his microphone and spoke quietly. "Sea Trek, this is Dragon Flower. Over."

"It's about time," the captain's gravelly voice came over the speakers.

"We're here. Send your barge to pick up the cargo."

"Roger that."

The trucks pulled up near the surf line and waited. In a few minutes, the ancient, World War II era landing craft approached.

"Get unloaded," the leader shouted.

Men from the trucks jumped to the beach and unfastened the canvas covering on their truck beds.

They unloaded heavy white bales. The men struggled under the weight of their cargo. Each bale contained over forty-four pounds of white powder.

The landing craft ran up on the beach and dropped its loading ramp. The men made like ants, and each carried a bale onto the boat. Then they returned for another load.

THE LOVINGLY RESTORED 1971 Chevrolet Impala convertible sat parked on the road above the beach. A tall (for a Vietnamese) colonel in an Army uniform emerged.

A UAZ-469 off road vehicle pulled in behind the Chevy. The 469 looked like an ugly offspring of an American Jeep and an old Dodge PowerWagon.

A captain in a Vietnamese Army uniform hopped out of the 469 and ran to the colonel. "Colonel Bao," he said, bowing slightly, "the radio is tuned in and ready to go."

"Are the troops in place?"

"All is set, sir."

Colonel Bao Van Doc rubbed the scar on his chin. *This is one transaction that will not go through.*

He raised his field glasses and watched the activity on the beach below. The men traipsed back and forth from their trucks to the landing craft. *Thank the gods I never had to do that.*

He looked farther out in the bay and saw the rust bucket lying at anchor. Two Vietnamese Navy patrol boats charged in from the open ocean.

"You may commence action, Captain," he said, lowering his glasses.

The captain stepped back to his vehicle and grabbed the microphone. He spit out a few words then watched the scene below unfold.

Four canvas-covered trucks with Army markings rumbled onto the beach. Each disgorged about twenty soldiers.

The gunfire exchange was brief. The smugglers quickly surrendered.

Bao watched the two patrol boats charge toward the tramp steamer. The old ship slipped her mooring and made for open sea. The patrol boats gave chase.

An uneven contest, the best the skipper could get out of his ancient ship was a puttering eight knots. The patrol boats easily made forty.

As the boats closed on the ship, the crew of the ship cast off a tarp covering a bump on the afterdeck revealing an American M2 machine gun. The gunners opened fire on the patrol boats. Fifty caliber bullets slammed into the hull and super structures of the one boat. Men fell.

The first patrol boat opened fire. The KOMAR-class motor torpedo boats were equipped with Styx anti-ship missiles.

An eruption of smoke and flame burst skyward from the starboard side of the first patrol boat, launching the missile into the air.

It only took seconds for the missile to find its target. The rusty steamer exploded into ten thousand tons of junk and debris.

From his lookout on the mountain, Colonel Bao smirked. *First obstacle gone.*

He looked down to the beaches. The ants were reversing their labor, carrying the bales back up the beach and loading them unto the trucks.

That's enough coke to supply the entire United States for a year.

Bao had no problem with supplying drugs to the Americans. *Let the bastards kill themselves. It's poetic justice.*

When the ants finished loading the trucks, the soldiers lined up the smugglers. On order from an officer on the beach, the soldiers opened fire. The smugglers crumpled to the beach, their bodies oozing blood into the white sand.

Bao smirked. *At high tide, their bodies will be washed out to sea where the sharks and the crabs can deal with them.*

12

PREPARATION — SEATTLE

The network operation center at Ted's office looked like the control room in the Johnson Space Center. Three rows of servers ran in the dark to the back of the large room. The room at the front of the server room was well lit.

Shelves hung from two walls at ninety-degree angles. On the shelves, which served as desks, half a dozen monitors sat with keyboards hung under the shelves. The action happened here. On a shelf above the desks, a dozen or more monitors showed the status of the various systems running.

Bear sat at one of the workstations. He was about Ted's height but built like a brick shit house. His bushy red hair and beard exploded in every direction, his belly hung over his pants. He pushed the granny glasses back on his nose. "Okay, compadre, he we go."

He typed an array of characters onto the green screen on his monitor. A box popped up that said, "Cracker Working..." A green bar at the bottom of the message box slowly moved from left to right.

"Have you ever done this before?" Ted asked as he stood over Bear's chair.

"Are you kidding? How stupid do you have to be to try to hack into the DOD?" He turned and grinned up at Ted.

"Whatever that level of stupidness is, I think we just hit it."

Ted and Bear first developed Cracker, a password cracking software years earlier while they worked at YTS Security. It had gone through many upgrades over the years.

Bear opened a prompt and typed in the path to Cracker. Then he entered his password and waited for the text message the app would send him to gain access.

Once the app was open, Bear entered the IP address of the Department of Defense network and pushed Enter. Bear sat back and whistled. "I hope they give us adjoining prison cells."

The green bar crept toward the right-hand side of the pop-up box. It hit the end of the space and another box popped up saying, "Complete. Push Ctrl-Alt-F10 to enter password."

Cracker deduced a safe password for the DoD network.

Ted pulled up a chair next to Bear. "Holy shit, Batman. You're in."

Bear swept his hand forward and took a bow. "You ask, I do."

Ted leaned forward toward the screen. "Okay, now how do we get to the satellite controls?"

"Take it easy, Pancho. We just got through the front door."

Bear continued to pound away at his keyboard. Occasionally, Ted stopped him and sent him off in other directions. They wandered blindly through the maze that was the DOD network until Bear found a link labeled "Space Force."

"I think we've got it." Bear looked up from the screen. "I read somewhere that the spy satellites were turned over to the Space Force."

Ted watched as Bear navigated through the Space Force site.

"Here we go." Bear beamed. "Satellites that fly over Southeast Asia."

"Find one that's over Vietnam."

"Of course, Captain Obvious."

Ted's heart pounded in his throat. He watched on the monitor next to Bear as a crystal-clear picture of Southeast Asia from one hundred miles up appeared.

"Zoom in."

Bear reached for his Diet Coke. The can was empty. "Damn. Okay, where we going?"

"Northeast Vietnam. I don't know if you can use place names, but it's in the Quang Binh Province"

Bear shook his head. "Nope. Doesn't look like it. We need to put in latitude and longitude."

Ted rolled across to another workstation. He typed in a few words and opened a website then typed in the province name.

"Looks like 22.410931 latitude, 104.586899 longitude."

"Okay, smart guy, let's see what we get."

Bear entered the coordinates. The screen in front of Ted zeroed in on the north central part of Vietnam. About seven hundred and fifty miles south of Hanoi, Quang Binh appeared on the screen.

"Looks like you got it," Ted said.

"Now what?"

"We've got to zoom in closer. Close enough to see the buildings on the ground."

Bear got up, walked to the mini-fridge and grabbed another can of Diet Coke. He snatched a bag of Cheetos from a shelf.

"Oh, God. Not Cheetos again," Ted said. "You know how long it took me to clean the orange crap off my keyboard last time?"

"You gotta feed genius. No fuel, no work." Bear settled back into his chair.

The image on the screen enlarged. Ted could see the thick jungle canopy. Occasionally, he made out roads. A few villages were scattered here and there.

Ted pointed to the screen. "It's a big area. The closer we zoom in, the less we can see at one time."

"It may take us some time. I just hope the DOD doesn't detect us waltzing around in here before we find what you want."

Four Diet Coke cans and several snack bags later, Ted raised his hand. "Stop. I think we got it." He tapped on the screen.

Bear slid over next to him and poked his hairy head near the monitor. "What? What do you see?"

"Right here?" He pointed to four rectangular shapes on the edge of the screen. "See, this looks like camouflaged buildings. One looks like a barracks. There's a fence of some sort around these two. Can you get in more?"

"Shucks, I can read the tags on their underwear if I want."

Bear scrolled in.

"Okay, stop," Ted said. "Look at this."

"That's gotta be it." Bear grinned from ear to ear. "No doubt that's a barbed-wire fence. This building has all sorts of antennae on top of it. Must be a radio shack. This must be the barracks. Here's the camp office."

"Okay, we've found some sort of military camp. But is it *the* POW prison?"

Bear rolled his chair away. "I don't think you can determine that from these pictures. We can't just hang around in the DOD system. Someone will eventually discover us. You're gonna have to go and look for yourself."

Ted felt a chill run down his spine. "Let's keep looking. Just to be sure. No telling how many camps there might be in this neck of the woods."

A QUICK CALL to Allison Clarke, the CEO of Millennium Systems, did the trick. Several years earlier, Ted got Allison out of a jam that would have cost her ten years in the state penitentiary and through the ordeal they became fast friends. Even with all her money and power she treated Ted, with his incredible technical knowledge, as an equal.

Hope craned her head back and took in the world headquarters of Millennium Systems, which occupied the entire Millennium Tower at Fourth and Columbia in Seattle. The white Tower, built on a pedestal that gradually widened to cover the entire block, had a grass and tree-covered park at its base. The unusual building was often featured in architectural magazines.

"These guys certainly don't scrimp when it comes to their building, do they?" Hope asked. In the lobby, a fountain danced in front a two-story-tall modern art mural that she didn't comprehend.

They collected temporary ID badges at building security in the glass and marble lobby. The guard checked his list and gave Ted a key to the elevator. In the elevator bank, there was one elevator with a single stop, the executive office suite on the forty-fifth floor. Hope, Ted, Chris, and Kathy entered the cherrywood-and-brass-trimmed car. Hope watched her brother insert and turn the key. The express took only a moment to reach the top floor.

The elevator doors opened, and they stepped out into a posh lobby. Lush carpet lay under expensive, ivory-colored leather furniture. Oil paintings with little spotlights over them hung on the walls. Large plants filled the corners.

A semi-circular marble desk covered one wall, with two Barbie clones, a blonde and a brunette, wearing headsets, sitting behind flat-screen computer monitors. They wore tight-fitting business attire and spared no effort on their hair or makeup.

"Humph —" Hope mumbled to herself. "I don't think they were chosen for their SAT scores. I wonder who in HR hired these two?"

Ted leaned into his little sister's ear and whispered, "Allison always did have an eye for the ladies."

He walked up to the desk and said, "Ted Higuera and company here to see Allison Clarke."

"Mr. Higuera, she's expecting you. If y'all will just come this way, please." The tall blonde rose from her chair and led them down the hallway.

Hope shook her head as the woman led the way. The receptionist opened an oak-framed glass door. "Mr. Higuera and friends, Ms. Clarke."

"Ted, Kathy, Chris, good to see you." Allison emerged from behind her desk, hand outstretched. She turned to Hope, "I'm Allison Clarke." As always, she wore an expensive business suit over her petite frame. That day it was accented by a silk scarf held in place with a diamond brooch.

"Hi. I'm Hope Higuera."

"Oh, yes. I've been to your restaurant." She took Hope's hand in both of hers.

Kathy gaped out the windows. "Wow! What a view."

A glass wall looked out over Elliot Bay and Puget Sound with the snow-covered Olympic Mountains across the water. The adjoining wall looked toward the south. Mount Rainier towered over the Cascade Range like a giant snow cone.

"We got lucky with nice weather today," Allison said.

Allison's office was gigantic, bigger than the house Hope shared with Mama and her little brother and sister. The ceiling was two stories tall. A mezzanine lined two walls of the office, with floor-to-ceiling bookcases, coffee tables, and overstuffed chairs. It reminded Hope of the library in the mansion in some English TV series.

Hope looked at the loveseats on either side of a glass-topped coffee table.

"Don't bother sitting." Allison waved toward the door. "We're going downstairs to R&D."

Hope noticed Kathy transfixed in front of an oil painting of a ballerina tying her shoes.

"Is this —?" Kathy stopped in mid-sentence.

"Yes. All three of them are Degas."

Hope noticed two other ballerina pictures on the adjoining wall.

"Wow," Kathy whispered.

Allison led them to the elevator where she swiped her ID badge against a reader. "One of the perks of office. I get a private elevator. You could spend the rest of your life waiting for elevators in a building this tall."

Hope's ears popped as the elevator dropped forty-eight floors. When the door opened, they were in a different world.

Gone were the trappings of power and office. They stepped into a sealed-off lobby. It could have been a bank vault. The only feature was a heavy steel door with a mirror in the top half. Allison stepped to a high-tech bio-metric reader and placed the palm of her right hand against the device. A red light flashed under her hand, like the barcode scanner in a supermarket, emitting a slight hum. The light turned from red to green. Allison entered a number on a keypad and a buzzer sounded above the door.

"Come on in. That's step one." Allison said while the door opened.

Through the door they entered a glassed-in foyer. On the other side of the heavy glass wall, an armed security guard sat behind a desk. There was a pass-through and a small, round, metal grill in the glass, like at the box office of a movie theater, to allow communication.

"Good afternoon, Mrs. Clarke. What's the weather like outside?"

Hope choked down a retaliatory comment on the guard's use of "Mrs." Allison showed no sign of insult.

"You're missing a sunny day, Paul." Allison turned to Ted and Chris. "We have a running joke about Paul spending his life in a cave down here." She turned back to the guard. "We need access to conference room five, and when are you going to start calling me Allison?"

"Whatever you like, Mrs. Clarke. Please sign in." Paul pushed a clipboard through the opening above his desk, a smirk on his face.

Allison signed the crew in, then walked to a glass door and swiped her ID badge.

"Isn't that a little over-kill?" Hope asked.

"You can't be too careful." Allison held the door for her visitors. "We build our competitive advantage down here. You'll need to swipe your cards as you pass through the door and do a hand scan, too."

Hope felt a little silly as she held her hand over the bio-metric scanner. Why did they need her handprint?

As if she read Hope's thoughts, Allison said, "We handprint everyone who goes through a class-one security checkpoint."

Allison led them down a long white hallway with a blue stripe at waist-level, a faint scent of antiseptic in the air. At every door, there was at least a card reader. On some of the doors, there were bio-metric scanners. "We record every person who goes through a door down here." Allison stopped in front of a heavy-looking door. "We have RFID chips in our ID badges. Our system knows where you are every second you're in the building."

She scanned her palm again, swiped her card, and entered a password on a keypad. "This is our highest level of security. No one goes in here unless they have a reason. Including the CEO. Our CSO will receive a report in the morning of everyone who passed through a class-one security checkpoint."

Except for a stainless steel table with several white cardboard boxes under it, the room was bare. Standing next to the table, a small Indian man in a lab coat nodded as they entered.

"Ms. Clarke, right on schedule as usual." He glanced at a high-tech-looking wristwatch.

"When am I ever going to get you to start calling me Allison?" Allison turned to Ted. "You remember Gopi Singnapoora don't you?" She turned to the other three. "Gopi is our chief Technical Officer (CTO)."

"Gopi?" Hope asked.

"My full name is much too long for you to pronounce, Ms. Higuera." Gopi spoke with a slight accent. He shook their hands, then motioned toward the table. "Ms. Clarke wanted me to give you a demo."

Gopi pulled four piles of high-tech looking material and helmets from the boxes.

"This is a top-secret project we're working on for the Defense Advanced Research Projects Agency, DARPA," Allison said. She picked up the closest pile of material and shook it out to reveal a Star Trek-looking body suit.

"I give you the future of covert combat operations." Gopi swept his hand toward the table with a flourish. "This suit will allow our operatives to go virtually anywhere unnoticed."

"Gopi likes to be a little melodramatic." Allison waved away Gopi's claim. "It's not just a combat suit; it has some of the most advanced technical components in the world." She handed a suit to each squad member. "You can change in the restrooms."

"Change —" Hope muttered.

"Yes. To really see what it's capable of, you need to be wearing it."

Hope held up her suit. It looked like a child-sized medium.

"I'll never get this on." Hope patted her ample hips. "May be someone like Kathy might squeeze into it."

"Don't worry, one size fits all." Allison smiled at Hope's concern.

The boys headed for the men's room without comment.

Hope muttered as she and Kathy headed for the ladies. All her life she cursed her curvaceous measurements. *How the hell am I going to get my hips, much less my freak-show boobs, into this thing?*

THE DRUG WAR — VIETNAM

T he ancient flatbed truck backed onto the beach and six
men jumped out. They laughed and joked as they
launched two pangas into the surf.

Two men stood beside each panga lifting the bow into the
waves while the third took the wheel at the little steering console.
The men grunted and pushed, and the boat slipped slowly back
into the water. The men at the controls fired up the big, black
Mercury outboards and lowered them into the water. The
propellers caught hold and the boats slid backward. The men at
the bows clambered aboard.

The white fiberglass pangas with blue interiors were twenty-
five feet long powered by a 225 horsepower outboard motor.

As soon as there was water under their keels, the boats spun
and raced to open water. Both boats were capable of twenty-five
knots and soon were out of sight of land.

A small freighter appeared on the horizon. The boats drew
close, and the freighter dropped heavy lines for the pangas.

The boat crews quickly attached the lines fore and aft and the
boats came to rest in the lee of the freighter.

A head appeared above the freighter's bulwarks thirty feet

above the pangas. "You got the money?" English was obviously not the captain's first language.

From the forward boat, a short, heavy man with a thick beard yelled back. "Si, Señor. I have it here."

A quarter-inch line dropped from the freighter. "Send it up. You better have all of it."

The squat man pulled a duffle bag from the compartment in the bow and tied it to the line.

Men on deck hauled the line up. After a moment the captain leaned over the bulwark again. "OK, get ready to receive your cargo."

Electric engines whirled and cargo booms hoisted two pallets over the side and lowered the pallets into the pangas. The pangas cast off.

With the load on board, the pangas rode much deeper in the water and their speed was cut to fifteen knots.

After two hours, the pangas ran up on the beach. The helmsmen expertly gunned the engine and, at the last minute, raised them out of the water to keep the propellors out of the sand.

The men jumped from the boats and hauled them as far ashore as they could, then began unloading them.

Four men with AK-47 assault rifles climbed from the truck and covered the operation.

The men carried the heavy bundles to the truck, then went back for more. Soon the cargo was all in the truck.

Machine gun fire exploded on the beach. Before the guards had time to react, they were cut down.

The six boatmen ran for cover. Three were slaughtered on the beach. One dived under the truck. The other two made it to a panga. They shoved it out into the water and scrambled aboard. Before they had time to fire up the engine, their bodies were riddled with red holes.

Six men with automatic weapons rose from the sand dunes

and carefully moved forward. They checked each body to make sure the victims were dead.

The sixth boatman huddled under the truck in fear.

The leader of the gunmen noticed him. "Paco, get that *pendejo* out from under the truck," he said in Spanish.

The last boatman was pulled out and stood up. The leader walked up to him and stood fact-to-face.

"Hey, *cabrón*, who is this load for?"

"I don't know, *Señor*. We just bring it in from a ship offshore."

The leader smashed his gun's butt into the boatman's stomach.

The boatman screamed and sank to his knees. "I promise, *Señor*. I have a family."

The leader kicked him in the head. "Who was this for?"

The boatman's tears blurred his vision. He held his belly and weakly said, "La Reina, *Señor*. I swear."

The leader shot him in the head.

14

CAT SUITS — SEATTLE

T ed and Chris spent so much time together in locker rooms over the years that neither felt any embarrassment over undressing and suiting up.

"What kind of game is this?" Chris asked as he put his leg through the head hole in the one-piece suit.

Ted was a little discombobulated pulling the skin-tight suit on by putting his legs into the head hole. He was amazed at how the fabric stretched to let him in.

"Holy *caca*, Chris. These threads might fit."

He got his feet through the legs and pulled his arms into the sleeves. He fiddled around with his crotch until he got comfortable.

"These too?" Chris asked, pointing at a pair of boots sitting on the floor next to the bench.

"I guess so." Ted picked up the closest set. "Uh, I think these are for you." They were a size 13. He took the smaller pair and slipped them on.

"Hey, this is great. You can hardly tell you're wearing shoes."

When they re-entered the meeting room, Hope and Kathy were already there.

Kathy took Ted's breath away. When dressed in civilian clothes, she looked like a stick girl. But with the body-hugging suit, he could see her subtle curves.

She reminded him of a Siamese cat. Long slender waist, rounded behind, short legs, and small breasts. For some reason, he couldn't take his eyes off her.

He had not been interested in any woman since his fiancée, Maria, ran off to Mexico with their unborn son to take over her father's drug empire. She had not allowed him any contact with his boy. In the intervening years he lived like a monk and pined for her every day.

"Okay, kids." Gopi clapped his hands together. "It's time to show you what these babies will do."

Without warning, Gopi pulled an automatic pistol from a drawer in the table and fired three shots at Ted.

Ted stumbled back and grabbed his chest. No blood. It hurt where the bullets impacted, but no damage done.

"As you can see, these suits are bullet-proof. Any small arms bullets will just bounce off. But don't get too cocky. A fifty-caliber round will tear you apart."

He handed Ted a helmet. "Go ahead, put this on."

It looked like a golden motorcycle helmet with the Millennium Systems logo on each side and a clear plastic faceplate over the eye opening. He noticed the word "Ted" over the faceplate. He slipped on the helmet.

"It works just like your cybernetic sunglasses, Ted." Gopi patted Ted on the shoulder. "Start the computer."

"Uh — okay." Ted cleared his throat. "Computer."

"Good morning, Ted. How may I help you?" A female voice seemed to originate in his head. For years he'd been using the Delphi sunglasses that Allison had given him. They were the most sophisticated computing device on earth.

"You'll notice, Ted, that the helmet responds to all commands that your Delphi does." Allison smiled at him. "But there's a lot more sophistication built into it."

She pressed a button on the wall. "Computer, display cyber helmet tutorial."

Ted removed the helmet.

A screen dropped from the ceiling and came to life. After a brief splash screen with the Millennium Systems logo, it switched to a three-D shot of the helmet.

"GOOD MORNING, Ted, Chris, Hope and Kathy," the computer simulation said. Today I'm going to give you a brief overview of the Covert Action Technology (CAT) suit. This outfit was developed with careful collaboration between DARPA, that's the Defense Advanced Research Projects Agency, the Department of Defense, Millennium Systems, the University of Washington, and the Massachusetts Institute of Technology."

The helmet on the screen slowly rotated three hundred sixty degrees. "This combat outfit was designed to the most exacting specifications and will give our operatives an unparalleled advantage in the field."

"Yeah, so how come I feel like Bozo the Clown wearing this?" Ted mumbled.

"The cyber helmets can transmit and receive via geo-synchronous military satellites. They use laser beams to broadcast and receive, ensuring no lag time in any conditions. The built-in cameras let the controllers see and hear what the operatives are experiencing in the field."

Ted felt around on his helmet for a camera but couldn't find any.

"With these communications, you have access to any database or application in the world. All data stored are in a secure Defense Department cloud."

Chris shook his head. "Jesus God. What'll they think of next?"

"I'm glad you asked that, Chris," the simulation said. "The

helmets control the CAT. You have temperature control. The chameleon color control allows the suit to blend in with any environment, rendering you virtually invisible. The suit is bulletproof and quick drying."

"Wow," Chris said. "That's just like the movie *Predator*."

"We almost named the suit the Predator," Gopi responded.

"How are these things powered?" Ted asked.

"Ted, they are run by special batteries developed by Tesla for this application." A picture of a battery approximately the size of a playing card showed on the screen. "These batteries are good for twelve hours."

The picture changed to a webbed belt with several accessories. "I would like to direct your attention to your utility belts. Please put them on."

The four picked up the belts and put them on.

"First of all, you will notice the holster on the belt," the computer said. "It holds an experimental Colt Model 2021. This pistol has a built-in silencer and can fire bullets, explosive shells, and tranquilizer darts. The magazines for the bullets are color coded red, the magazines for the tranquilizers are blue, and the explosive shells are purple. There are extra batteries on the belt."

"My mother always taught me to accessorize," Hope said.

"Yeah, you really know how to get to a girl," Kathy answered.

"You will notice that the entire outfit is capable of changing colors to match your surroundings," the computer went on. The screen changed to a solid purple. The CAT suits changed to purple too. Then the screen went to a jungle scene and a desert scene. The suits changed color to match. "If you lift your lenses, your eyes will be visible, but all the rest of you will be camouflaged."

"Holy crap, Allison." Ted removed his helmet. "These things are from some science-fiction movie."

Allison laughed. "You might be surprised what your government spends your taxes on." She took Ted's helmet. "We built ten of these suits. They cost billions. DARPA has five of them and we retained five for testing."

"Wait a minute." Chris said. "We are only four. Where's the other one?"

Allison grinned. "Oh, it's undergoing field tests right now."

"I'm not comfortable with this," Kathy said. "I can see the use for the suits, but I'm not going to carry a gun. We can't just shoot our way through a foreign country."

"Don't worry," Ted said. "We hope we never need them, but as an old friend of mine once said, 'It's better to have them and not need them than to need them and not have them.'"

Kathy shook her head. "I'm sorry, Ted. No go. I won't carry a gun and I don't think any of you should either."

"Miss Nguyen to see you, Mr. Ted," Abiba said in her British accent.

Ted had long since given up on his receptionist ever calling him just Ted.

"Great, show her back."

He smiled as he watched the pair glide through the sea of cubicles toward him. Kathy was barely five feet tall and slender. Abiba was a huge black woman from Ethiopia. Over six feet tall and approaching 300 pounds. Abiba moved like a ballerina, her feet hardly touching the ground.

"Hi, Kathy. Welcome aboard." Ted gestured for Kathy to enter his office.

He watched her look around. His cherry desk and credenza were a big upgrade from the old Army surplus desk he first occupied.

"Your office seems different from what I remembered," Kathy said.

"We had to rebuild the whole mezzanine after the terrorist fire-bombed us."

Kathy stopped and stood in front of a six-foot tall poster of Spiderman swinging through the canyons of New York. "Spider-man?" she asked.

"Yep. Look at the signatures. Stan Lee and Steve Ditko. That picture's got to be worth some money now."

"Where did you ever get it?"

Ted smiled and gestured to Kathy to sit down. "I won it at Comic-Con in San Diego a long time ago."

Ted sat behind his desk, and Kathy took one of the uphol-stered chairs in front of it. Ted said, "Kathy, the reason I wanted to see you is to make sure you know what you're getting into. This isn't some Club Med vacation to Vietnam."

"I know. But to do what you want to do, which I still think is stupid, you need me. I speak the language and am familiar with the culture. My dad'll come with us as far as Hanoi. He still has contacts in Vietnam that can help us." She paused and took a deep breath. "I think this whole idea is insane, but without me..." Her voice trailed off.

Ted looked at her determined eyes. He'd seen her in court a time or two and noticed that same predatory look. "I'm grateful." He shook his head and let out a deep sigh. "I don't know if the rumor is true, but if my uncle is alive, I'd never forgive myself for not trying."

"You can thank Chris for this," Kathy said. "He okayed the time off."

"He'd do anything for me," Ted said. "I saved his life years ago and we've been bonded at the hip ever since." Ted picked up a martial arts magazine and handed it to Kathy. "It could be dangerous. I understand that you don't want to carry a gun, but you should at least be able to defend yourself."

Kathy sneered. "You mean the big bad detective isn't going to protect me?"

Ted shook his head. "God protects she who protects herself."

He felt a flicker in his heart as she half-grinned at his comment. "At least let me take you to the gym and teach you the basics."

Kathy smiled. "Okay, Mister Superstar. Let's go."

"I'm GOING to show you some basic self-defense maneuvers from Krav Maga." They were in a padded gym, wearing their white karategi uniforms. "Krav Maga is a military self-defense and fighting system developed for the Israel Defense Forces derived from a combination of techniques sourced from boxing, wrestling, judo, aikido, and karate."

"Hmmm... Sounds deadly."

Ted couldn't tell what she was thinking, she had a deadpan face. "Okay, we're gonna start with learning how to escape an aggressor's hold." He took a couple of steps toward her and put his hands on her shoulders.

He felt his pulse quicken the moment he touched her. He looked in her eyes and saw her staring into empty space. Her mind was somewhere far away.

He pulled her slight body close to him. He outweighed her by at least eighty pounds. His breathing came fast and shallow. Their faces were inches apart. For a moment, Ted forgot why they were there. He wanted to take her in his arms and kiss those tender lips.

She stomped on his foot.

"Hey," Ted yelled.

She kneed him in the groin.

"Yow." Ted dropped his grip on her and grabbed his family jewels.

She launched a lightning kick to his chest that sent him reeling. Before he could recover, she grabbed his arm and flipped him over her leg, sending him to the floor.

Ted rolled over laughing. *How could I have thought that the*

Dragon Lady would ever be interested in me. He still held his groin. *I'm probably out of action for a month anyway.*

"Where the hell did you learn that?"

Kathy stood over him, smiling. "Oh, did I forget to tell you? My father insisted we all learn self-defense. I've been training since I was six. I have a black belt in Vo Viet Nam."

MARIA GONZALES, a good-looking red head in her early thirties, sat on a lounge chair by the pool. Her two-year-old son, Eduardo, splashed about in a kiddy pool. Maria finished adding a layer of sunscreen to her long legs and picked up her book.

This was a brief respite in her complicated life. Her business was a 24/7 concern. She might be called out at any hour of the night or day.

She looked at Eduardo and wished things could be different. He had never met his father. Ted was a good man. Everything she could ever want in a man, but her family business inserted a wedge between them that could never be overcome.

"*Señora*, I have bad news." The voice was in Spanish.

Maria looked over to the door. Martín, her ranch foreman stood with his hat in his hands.

"Come on out." Maria waved a hand at him. "What's happening?"

"Our shipment this morning was hijacked." Martin wiped his brow with his fingers. "We don't know who did it yet."

Maria's pale face turned red. "Well find out." She jumped to her feet. "We can't let something like this go unpunished. I'll destroy whoever had the nerve to attack one of my shipments."

"*Sí, Señora.*"

TED DROVE into the litter-strewn parking lot of the Dirty Bird. He'd been there several times before. Years ago, he did a job for the owner, Rico Caglione that kept Rico out of prison, at the time, and Ted knew that Rico owed him.

Rico was serving twenty-five to life for human trafficking. and his son, Rico Junior ran the club.

It was obvious that the club's clientele was protective of their identities. The building was in the front of the lot, the parking lot behind the building. The main entrance, in the back of the building, was shielded from the street. Anyone entering or leaving would be unseen by passersby.

At that time of day, there was only a scattering of cars in the lot. Pickup trucks mixed with muscle cars, BMWs, and Mercedes.

"Hey, handsome, can I help you?" the gorgeous redhead in a black leather bustier asked as he entered. She had to be at least six feet tall. In four-inch stilettos, she towered over Ted's five-eight. *Hijole, the knockers on that lady poke clear into the middle of next week.*

His eyes adjusted as he looked around the dimly lit room. The walls and ceiling were painted black. A moldy odor wafted up from the cheap shag carpet under his feet. The aromas of beer, tobacco, and vomit assaulted his nose. Loud techno-rock blared from speakers on the walls. A stage with four stripper poles dominated the room, circled by a bar and chairs.

A couple of patrons sat at the bar, salivating over the skinny blonde in platform stilettos with gigantic boobs who strutted naked on the stage to Nine Inch Nails. In the harsh glare of the klieg light, Ted could see that the thatch of hair between her legs, while neatly trimmed, didn't match the hair on her head.

The rest of the room held tables and chairs. A few men sat at the tables, many accompanied by young women in lingerie. A slightly plump woman with enormous breasts twirled tassels in her customer's face.

"What can I do for you, honey?" The redhead rubbed her hands over Ted's shoulders.

Jerked back to reality by her touch, Ted remembered his task. "I'm here to see Mr. Caglione. I have an appointment."

"What's your name?"

"Ted Higuera."

"Come right this way, Mr. Higuera." She turned and strutted toward a door at the back of the room. Ted was mesmerized by her perfect ass. He hadn't been interested in any woman since Maria left him, but he wasn't dead.

Somehow, he managed to notice the other women in the room.

There's enough silicone in here to fill Malibu Beach.

"Mr. Caglione, we have a young stud here to see you." The redhead opened the door and stepped aside.

Caglione's office was the height of good taste. Carpeted, with dark wood-paneled walls and walnut furniture, the walls covered with English hunting pictures like an expensive gentlemen's club. Someone had spent a lot of money on an interior designer.

Junior Caglione rose from behind the huge desk and extended his hand. "Mr. Higuera. My father speaks highly of you." Caglione wore silver slacks that were so tight Ted could tell his religion. He wore a white silk shirt with the first three buttons open. A gold chain with a cross hung around his neck.

Sure different from your father. Old Rico was Saville Row all the way.

Ted shook Caglione's hand. "I need a favor. Your father did this for me once before." Ted sat in the chair Caglione waved to. "Several years ago, when we had a case in Mexico, your dad supplied us with firearms on the other side of the border."

"I kinda think I remember that." Caglione sounded like a spoiled Millennial punk. "So what do you need now?"

Ted gulped. Here was the big ask. "Do you have any connections in Vietnam?"

Caglione studied Ted for a moment. "Uh... yeah... sure. I have a dude I do business with over there."

Ted didn't want to ask what kind of business. "We're going on a little vacation to Vietnam. It might get a little messy. We're gonna need our baggage smuggled into the country." Ted paused to let it sink in.

Caglione showed no reaction.

"Can you help me?"

Caglione flipped a non-existent piece of thread from this cuff. He studied Ted for a long moment. "I know my old man trusted you, but I don't know you."

Ted swallowed. "Listen, Junior... may I call you that...?"

Caglione nodded.

"... You won't have any trouble from me. What we're going for is not necessarily sanctioned by the State Department." There was a long pause. "I'd owe you a big one."

There was no expression on Caglione's face. "You sure would."

"Money's not a problem. We'll pay whatever the price is."

Caglione grinned. "Let me see what I can do."

15

DRUG PROBLEMS — HANOI

Nguyen Phuong Nga, the Vietnamese Foreign Ministry spokeswoman, stood in front of a bank of microphones. She looked out and saw the TV cameras and the crush of reporters.

Reports of horrible conditions in the drug rehabilitation centers in Vietnam dominated the headlines. She needed to do something to show that her country was a modern, compassionate nation.

"Reports of inhumane conditions in our drug rehabilitation centers are groundless," she began. "The government's primary goal with all the offenders is rehabilitation. We want those individuals subject to this horrible illness to recover and become productive members of society."

The crowd of reporters murmured, and several raised their hands and shouted questions.

Nga ignored them. "Our rehabilitation programs are humane, effective, and beneficial for drug users, the community, and society."

Once again, the reporters shouted questions. "Nga, what about the reports that you use these inmates as slave labor?"

"Vietnam's drug rehabilitation centers comply with Vietnamese law and are in line with drug-treatment principles set by the U.S., the U.N., and the World Health Organization. You will find none of the kinds of things that have been reported there."

"I'M SICK. I NEED A FIX." Hanh Kim Phuong, a university student with a habit, clutched his arms around himself. At his side, Mai, a computer science major, held her arms around herself too as she shook. His dealer, a well-dressed kid known on the campus as Easy sat on the shelf of a raised flower bed.

"You got money for me?"

"Yeah, here." Phuong handed him a wad of bills.

Easy counted the money, nodded and said, "Okay." He reached in his pocket and produced two small Zip-Lock bags containing white powder.

"You're under arrest." Two plainclothes policemen grabbed Phuong and Mai before they could move. "Come with us."

They hauled the couple to a waiting car. Easy remained on his perch at the flower bed counting the money.

PHUONG AND MAI were taken to the local police station and shoved into a small room.

"Remove your clothes," the overweight guard demanded. Mai looked at Phuong.

"No," she said.

The guard slapped her across the face. Mai staggered back. The guard grabbed her by the shirt and pulled it open. "I said undress."

The other guard poked at Ngoc with an electric prod. "You, too, Romeo."

Ngoc took off his jacket and unbuttoned his shirt.

Mai gave him a forlorn look.

"Go ahead, Mai. We don't have any choice."

The young lovers were soon naked in front of the guards.

Another male guard came into the room. "You first," he said to Phuong. "Bend over that chair."

Phuong submitted to the body cavity search.

"You're next," the guard said to Mai.

Mai stood in the corner with her hands covering her breasts.

"I said NOW."

"Nice ass," the first guard said as he turned Mai around. "Bend over the table."

She bent over the table and the guard donned a pair of surgical gloves.

"Now, let's see what you're hiding."

He poked his fingers up her vagina.

She shrieked. It hurt. She felt him feel around inside of her.

He pulled his fingers out and spread her cheeks. "Okay, now the other hole."

He poked his fingers into her anus.

"Oh, God!" It felt like he had stuck a red-hot poker in her.

After they were finished, the guards examined the prisoner's mouths using wooden sticks to move the tongue around.

"They're clean," the first guard said.

The second guard tossed them each a set of gray pajamas. "Get dressed."

The pair were pushed into a cell with thirty or forty other people their age.

"Phuong, I can't do this." Mai shook over her whole body. "I need to pee."

There was one stainless steel toilet/sink combination on the back wall. The toilet overflowed and the whole cell smelt of sewage.

"Don't worry. Your father will get us out of here."

She could hardly think, but she knew her father owned a small factory that made athletic shoes. He should have the pull to bail them out.

They were given no opportunity to use a telephone.

They spent the night huddled together on the floor against a wall. They were lucky to get a wall. Several other inmates fought over spots on the wall. The others got what sleep they could sitting on the floor. There was no room to spread out.

Mai wrapped her arms around herself, hugged tightly, and shivered. Tears rolled down her cheeks. "Phuong, I'm sick. I can't stand it."

"I know. Me, too." He was as pale as an English preacher. Sweat rolled down his forehead. Like most of the other inmates, he shook violently.

"What are we going to do?"

"Just hold on, baby. Hold on. This can't last forever."

In the morning, the residents of the cell were hustled into the back of a truck. They got no breakfast and no chance to use the facilities.

The truck was more crowded than the cell. The inmates stood as the truck bumped down the road. People couldn't hold it any longer and wet patches appeared on their clothes. A couple of inmates soiled themselves and the back of the truck reeked.

After two and a half hours of the torturous ride, the truck came to a halt and the doors opened.

Six armed soldiers bade the inmates to climb down.

Mai had never been so embarrassed. The front of her pants were soaked.

The soldiers separated the men from the women. Mai marched off with the other females. Phuong never saw her again.

Phuong's group of men marched into a detention center. There they gave their names and showed their ID. Clerks behind long tables took their information down.

An Army officer entered the room. "You are all here as drug

abusers. You will be assigned to jobs in the factory and will work for your keep."

"Wait a minute," Phuong shouted out. "You can't put us in prison without a trial."

A guard smacked Phuong in the kidney with his rifle butt.

"I can do anything I like." The officer smirked. "You are drug abusers. You are not entitled to a trial. You are all automatically sentenced to two years hard labor. Here you will get over your dependence and return to society as useful citizens."

The guards chuckled to themselves.

Phuong was taught to use a machine that cut the soles for flip-flops from large rubber sheets. Work was twelve hours a day. After work, each inmate got a bowl of rice and listened to an indoctrination lecture to learn how to be good communists. Then they were given another lecture on the horrors of drug abuse, and returned to their cells to grab what little sleep they could.

ON TO VIETNAM — SEATTLE

T ed lay on the floor mat and looked up into those mysterious eyes.

"Are you dead?" Kathy asked.

"Mmmm . . ." Ted replied.

He sat up, and Kathy turned and walked to the far side of the mat. "You ready to go again?"

Ted watched her as she walked away, mesmerized. She had a lean body. Asian women always reminded him of graceful cats when they moved. *I am Siamese if you please . . .*

He hadn't thought that way of another woman since Maria banished him from her life. He had asked Maria to marry him, and she disappeared into Mexico. When he tracked her down, he found that, after her father's murder, she had taken control of his drug cartel.

She exiled Ted from her life. The worst part was that she was carrying his baby. His son must be two years old. Ted had never seen him, never talked to him.

"Planet Earth to Ted. Are you in there?"

"Uh . . . yeah. Sorry. I just had my head rattled a little."

"Maybe we should knock off for today."

Ted met Kathy at the gym three days a week after work. She was an excellent sparring partner. She had him flat on his back as often as he beat her. Besides, he felt a spark of electricity between them every time they made contact.

While Ted showered, he thought, *Am I really getting interested in Kathy? What would Mama think if I brought a Vietnamese girl home?*

Ted's mother lived through the Vietnam War era. She had an unshakeable dislike for the Vietnamese and would never condone the relationship.

Am I really starting to like her? I know I'll never see Maria again; I'll never see my son.

He dried himself off and donned a light blue polo shirt and jeans. While he laced up his sneakers, his mind drifted back to Maria.

How do you solve a problem like Maria? he sang in his mind. *I know I owe nothing to Maria, but can I really start a relationship with Kathy?*

THE COST of airline tickets from Seattle to Hanoi was outrageous. Ted finally found a flight from Seattle to New York to Qatar to Hanoi at a reasonable cost. He dipped into the family's lottery winnings to pay for five tickets.

Then there was the travel time. With all the layovers and traveling three quarters of the way around the world, it took fifty-eight hours to reach Vietnam.

The flight from Seattle to JFK was unspectacular. They were jammed into a small jet operated by Spirit Airlines. The seats looked as if they came out of go-karts. The gay flight attended gave the safety speech.

"If the cabin loses pressure, the masks will fall from the overhead. Put the mask over your face and swipe your credit card. If your card is declined, tough luck."

The rest of the flight was no better. There were no snacks and they had to pay for any drinks they wanted.

When they reached New York, the world changed. They flew in a Qatar Air Airbus 380. Big and roomy, it offered excellent service.

Chris and Ted's sister, Hope, sat to his left. To his right were Kathy and her father, Chun. Chun forced his way onto the trip because he had the contacts in Vietnam and, Ted assumed, because he didn't want to let his daughter out of his sight. He and Kathy could both serve as translators.

Ted's knee rubbed against Kathy's. He felt that spark that he kept bottled up inside. Just the touch of her set his heart beating.

Damn, she's a fine-looking woman. Her long, shiny black hair and deep dark eyes set his heart afire. But was it fair for him to pursue her? His heart belonged to Maria. It always would. And he had to find a way to meet his son.

The plane touched down at 11:08 am Hanoi time. The hundreds of passengers were herded off the plane and lined up in customs. Ted's team only had carry-on bags.

The rest of the team cleared customs easily.

The officer scanned Ted's passport. "I'm sorry, sir, I'm going to have to ask you to step aside."

Wha...?

Ted walked to the box outlined on the floor with red tape that the officer indicated then a female officer led him to a room furnished only with a folding table and plastic chairs.

"What is the purpose of your visit?" she asked.

"Tourism. We're here with a friend who was born here and wants to show us the country."

She studied Ted's passport, then worked with the tablet in her hands.

"If you'll excuse me, sir, someone will be right with you."

What the hell is going on?

The wait was interminable.

After more than forty-five minutes, the door opened.

A slender man in a Vietnamese Army uniform wearing wire rimmed glasses perched on a long, narrow nose stood in the door. With close-cropped hair and piercing eyes, he walked as if he had a broom stick up his butt. The man just stared at Ted for over a minute, then came in and shut the door.

He set Ted's passport and a file folder on the table. "Mr. Higuera. . ." He horribly mis-pronounced Ted's name. "I am Colonel Bao Van Duc. You are on our watch list." He sat down opposite Ted.

"What? . . . why?" Ted shook his head. *What the hell have I gotten into now?*

"I ask the questions here." His English sounded like someone who had graduated from Oxford.

Is it the CAT suits? Have they interdicted them?

"How long do you plan to spend in Vietnam?"

Ted thought for a moment. "Uh . . . two weeks."

The colonel had a tick on the left side of his mouth. Every time it contracted; he rubbed his cheek. "And what do you plan on doing during those two weeks?"

Ted frowned. "Sightseeing. We're with my fiancée's father. He was born here. He wants to show us the old country." *Keep your lies close to the truth.*

"And what is your itinerary?" The colonel leaned forward resting his elbows on the table.

"I don't have it. Chun does. Let me think . . . from here we're going to Ha Dong I think, then Yen Bai. Those are the only names I remember."

"You have come a very long way to not know where you're going."

Ted took a deep breath and closed his eyes. Then he let the air out, opened his eyes and looked directly into the colonel's eyes. "I'm just along for the trip. My fiancé's father wants to show us his country. We'll go wherever he takes us."

The interview went on for over an hour. Colonel Bao asked

the same questions over and over again. Ted kept his story straight.

"Wait here, please, Mr. Higuera," the colonel finally said. It wasn't a request.

The colonel picked up his papers and left the room.

Several minutes later, the woman officer returned. She handed Ted his passport. "You may go now." She stood at the door and waited for Ted to exit.

Ted looked over his shoulder as he walked down the hallway and spied Colonel Bao staring at him, cell phone to his ear.

Chris and the gang were waiting in the lounge for him.

"What the hell was that about?" Chris asked before Ted finished crossing the room.

"Hell, if I know." Ted took a chair and waved at the server. "A Margarita please, on the rocks."

"What did they ask you, *hermano*?" Hope asked. Ted and Hope kept the Spanish to a minimum when they were with English speakers.

"They wanted to know why I was here, where I was going. They had a full-ass colonel come in and do the questioning."

Chun leaned close and whispered, "Mr. Ted, I have a bad feeling about this. Why would they pick you out of all the people on that plane?"

"Maybe it's no big deal, Dad." Kathy grabbed her father's arm. "Maybe they do this kind of stuff as a routine check."

Chun shook his head. "Vietnamese never do anything without a good reason. They are watching Ted."

Ted got his Margarita and took a deep sip. "Jesus Christ, are we marked already?"

CHUN LEFT the young people at the airport and caught a bus to stay with friends. Ted and company grabbed a Gab, the Vietnamese version of Uber, to their hotel.

The Golden Silk Hotel was in the old part of town. Far from the towering skyscrapers, the seven story French Colonial style building was the tallest in the neighborhood. From the outside, the white painted building looked rather plain with matching wrought iron railings and varnished teak cap-rails around the balconies.

The lobby looked like something from an Indiana Jones movie. The wicker furniture and hand-stitched silk cushions in the lobby jumped out at Ted. The front desk had brown and white checkered ceramic tiles on its front and teak trim. The whole place smelled of teak, the rich, warm, slightly spicy aroma hung in the air. A huge silk painting of a gnarled old tree filled the wall behind the front desk.

"Higuera, party of four," Ted said as he approached the desk.

A well-dressed young man typed something into his computer. "Ah, yes . . . Mr. Higuera." He mispronounced Ted's name horribly. It sounded more like Hee-goo-wa. "We have two rooms for you."

Ted leaned on the beautiful teak woodwork. "Two rooms? I asked for three."

"No, no," the young man said. "I have you down as two couples. Two rooms with king-sized beds. You will be most comfortable."

"But, Kathy and I need separate rooms . . . "

Kathy grabbed Ted's arm. "It's all right. Just go with the flow."

"No, it's important." Ted turned to the clerk. "You have to find us a third room"

"I'm sorry Mr. Hee-goo-wa, we are totally booked. There is no other room." His face changed like a light bulb went on over his head. "Perhaps I can find you room in another hotel?"

Hope stepped forward. "It's okay. Kathy and I can share one room and the boys the other."

"Whoa, there, cowgirl," Chris interjected. "I've spent enough nights listening to Higuera's snoring. I came on the trip to have time alone with you. Let them figure it out."

The clerk rang a bell and handed the room keys to a bellboy who immediately headed to the elevator.

Ted shook his head and followed.

Ted had chosen the hotel for its bargain prices. The rooms were only twenty-four U.S. dollars a night. He was overwhelmed with the opulence of the place.

He could envision beautiful Vietnamese women in evening gowns, handsome men in tuxes, and the occasional foreigner sitting at the bar. It was like something out of a '30s movie.

The cramped elevator took them to the top floor, leaving their luggage for the next trip. The bellboy opened the door to Chris and Hope's room. It was amazing. Everything was done in Chinese red. The huge bed had a fiery bedcover and red silk pillows.

They left Chris and Hope to explore and moved next door to Ted and Kathy's room.

"It's gorgeous," Kathy said as they stepped inside.

The room was done in light gray and white. The curtains on the windows were navy blue silk. Everywhere on the walls were silk paintings. Pictures of ponds, fish, flowers, and trees were of first quality.

On the dresser were a plate of fresh fruit and a bottle of Cabernet Sauvignon with two crystal glasses.

"Wha . . .?" Ted mumbled.

"Compliments of the house," the bellboy said. "Let us make up for the miscommunication." All the hotel staff seemed to speak perfect English, although none of them could pronounce Ted's name correctly.

A second bellboy showed up with their luggage.

Ted tipped the bellboys and closed the door after them.

"I should make up a fake name they can pronounce," Ted said.

Kathy laughed. "What are you going to use, my name?

Nguyen, is the most common name in Vietnam, but somehow I don't think it fits you."

"Well, I could always be Smith or Jones."

"You don't look like that either." She smiled and winked at him. "I think you better stick to a Spanish surname."

"I guess Higuera'll just have to do." He smiled back at her. "I'll sleep in the chair," Ted said, pointing at the over-stuffed chair by the windows.

"No, you won't." Kathy flashed him a smile. "We're big boys and girls. I think we can share the same bed without getting too cozy."

Ted held back a smile. "Let's get unpacked. What little we have."

He unzipped his carry-on. "Hold on," he whispered. "My bag has been searched."

"What? How...?"

"Shhh," Ted held a finger to his lips. "The place might be bugged," he mouthed.

"Did they take anything?" Kathy whispered.

Ted shook his head. "No, everything looks just like I packed it."

"Then how do you know it was searched?"

Ted smiled. "Spy craft. I attached a hair inside the zipper. It's not there now."

Kathy laughed. "Seen one to many James Bond movies, have we?"

Kathy searched her bag and found nothing missing, then went into the bathroom and returned with a piece of paper in her hand. "It's from Dad's friend. It was taped under the lid of the tank."

Ted moved closer to see what it said. It was in Vietnamese.

"It says that your friend from Seattle had the luggage shipped in. It will be delivered to this room tonight."

Junior Caglione got the cases past customs. Now Ted owed the mob a favor.

"I'm going to take a shower and freshen up, then we'll meet Chris and Hope in the bar." Kathy headed back to the bathroom with her backpack. Through the open door Ted could see a bidet next to the toilet. A wall-mounted phone was between the two accommodations.

Ted tossed his pack on the bed and opened the curtains. The full-length windows opened onto a small balcony. Ted stepped out and had a magnificent view of the old city.

He imagined it looked like this during the French colonization. Plaster-covered homes in all colors with tile roofs crowded together to fill the streets. There were no front yards. The doors opened onto the sidewalks.

He noticed a black Toyota sedan parked across from the hotel entrance in a no-parking zone. Two men sat inside.

People moved about everywhere. Crowds used the sidewalks and spilled over into the streets. Small cars sloughed through the traffic and crowds of people. Tiny trucks made their way through the mess. Motorbikes were everywhere. Zipping in and out of traffic and around all obstacles. One bike had a young man driving. A woman with a baby in her arms stood on the seat behind him. A boy not more than ten-years old sat on the seat behind her and clung to her legs.

Holy shit. They must have a death wish.

The sounds were too numerous to count; it just added up to overwhelming chaos. Vendors hawked their wares, people talking and shouting everywhere. The constant honking of horns, the revving engines of the motor bikes, and far in the background, the wailing of sirens.

A blue cloud hung over the city, and it smelled of gasoline.

Welcome to Vietnam, old buddy.

TED STARED as Kathy emerged from the bathroom. Clad in a blue silk dress with tiny yellow flowers, she combed her long black hair as she walked into the room.

"Ready to go?" she asked.

Ted continued to stare.

"Uh . . . planet Earth to Ted . . . "

"I'm . . . I'm sorry. My mind was elsewhere." *I better not tell her where it was. You're becoming an old coot.*

"Well get it back here. We need to meet Chris and Hope, and I have a special surprise."

"Uh . . . yeah. Give me a minute to change my shirt."

He ripped off the T-shirt and pulled a white turtleneck from his bag. He grabbed a black blazer and was ready.

"Okay, let's rock."

He opened the door for Kathy. She flowed like dancer rather than walked. He watched her from behind as she went down the hallway. The swaying of her hips mesmerized him.

Holy shit. What's going on?

The bar was straight out of *Indiana Jones and the Temple of Doom*. The room was done in dark teak. High-backed booths lined the perimeter. Glossy teak tables and chairs filled the center of the space. Behind the shiny bar, a mirror reflected the neat bottles of liquor. Male servers in tuxedos and females in skimpy dresses circulated through the crowd.

"Kathy," a shrill voice screamed.

Ted turned to see a tiny, even by Vietnamese standards, woman open her arms and run toward Kathy.

"Huong." Kathy grabbed the little woman and squeezed her tightly. They exchanged kisses on the cheeks.

"Ted, this is Huong," she said, as she released her grip and turned Huong toward Ted.

Ted held out his hand. "Delighted."

"Pleased to meet you, sir," Huong said.

Her hand was so tiny, Ted felt as if he was gripping a child.

"Oh, don't be so formal," Kathy chided. "This is just good, ol' Ted."

Chris and Hope arrived with guilty smiles on their faces and went through introductions.

"So, how did you two meet?" Ted asked as they crowded into one of the silk-upholstered booths.

"Huong went to the U-Dub." Kathy smoothed the back of her dress before sitting down. "We became best friends. We even lived together our senior year."

"I don't know what I would have done without Kathy," Huong said. "She introduced me to American life. I supposed if I hadn't met her, I would have spent four years hiding in corners."

"You must come from money," Chris said.

Hope poked him in the ribs with her elbow. "Don't mind him. He was raised by wolves."

Huong laughed. "It's no problem. Yes, my father owns several factories, and my uncle is the Minister of Security. I know that I live a privileged life. I just try to give back."

"She's dedicated to helping the common people," Kathy said.

A waiter appeared at the table. "Could I get you drinks?" he asked in perfectly accented English.

The group ordered and went back to conversations about college days.

"It's getting late," Kathy said, looking at her watch. "We better get some dinner."

"I have just the place," Huong said. "I have this all planned out."

THE NEW CENTURY — HANOI

Colonel Bao sat in the back of a white Toyota minivan. It might as well have been the bridge of the Star Ship Enterprise.

LCD monitors, microphones, keyboards, and CPUs surrounded Bao and two uniformed officers.

"Are we ready to go?" Bao asked.

The middle-aged man with a short gray haircut answered. "All units in place. All units checked in ready to go. We have five hundred officers at your command."

Bao nodded.

"It looks like we're going to need them. There are hundreds of people in that place. Maybe the fire marshal should do a little checking."

On the largest screen in the middle of the van, Bao saw hundreds of young people in party dress wriggling to the latest American dance tunes. *This is what they get for listening to decadent Western music.*

"All right. Give the word. GO!"

THE HOTTEST CLUB IN HANOI, the New Century Disco, catered to the young elite, as well as most of the foreigners in the city. Liquor flowed and well-dressed men and women offered products the club couldn't sell.

Molly, coke, H, speed, anything the heart desired. Beautiful young women in scanty dresses circulated through the crowd distributing the forbidden fruit.

Well-dressed young men attracted beautiful women and slowly they paired up. Many went upstairs to the private rooms.

Behind the bar, Than whirled and flipped bottles in the air as he prepared his signature cocktails. He moved to the music and sang as he worked. A half dozen young women sat at the bar and drooled.

A loud siren sounded. Uniformed and secret police burst through the doors. Everywhere people screamed.

The herd stampeded to the back door, where they were rounded up and hand-cuffed by the riot-gear-clad officers.

Others ran up the stairs, only to be herded back down by dozens of policemen.

More and more officers flooded the bar. Officers cuffed the patrons and lined them up against the walls. Anyone who offered resistance was clubbed with night-sticks.

Than dropped behind the bar. He slid open the door on a cabinet and climbed in.

Everywhere chaos reigned.

Colonel Bao walked into the room as if were on parade. He raised a bull horn to his lips. "Everyone, shut up! I want quiet."

His warning didn't seem to do any good. Uniformed officers with batons waded into the crowd bashing anyone who made noise.

This only increased the roar.

"Okay, Division One, you may start taking your prisoners to the vans."

A group of uniformed officers herded their charges out the door, night-sticks at the ready.

HOA AND NGOC huddled behind the sofa in a private room. Ngoc paid well for this room, but it was no big deal. His father owned the Toyota dealership in Hanoi.

Hoa squeezed as tightly into his arms as she could. Tears ran down her eyes and she whimpered and gasped.

"Be still. Maybe they won't find us."

"Ngoc, I'm ruined. If my father finds out I was here, he'll expel me from the family."

The door burst open.

Hoa and Ngoc slumped down even further and held their breaths.

They heard heavy boots stomping through the room.

"What have we here?" an officer said. He let out a little laugh. "A pair of love-birds."

He grabbed Hoa by the shoulder, tearing the arm off the dress that cost more than he made in a month.

"On your feet, children. Papa's taking you on a little trip."

Ngoc leapt to his feet. "No. You're making a mistake. My father is—"

He didn't finish the sentence. The policeman slammed his night-stick into Ngoc's stomach.

Ngoc folded over and collapsed to the floor.

"Now move it." The officer shoved Hoa toward the door.

The other policeman jerked Ngoc to his feet and shoved him after administering a quick kick to the butt.

THE POLICE STATION crawled with hundreds of well-dressed people, their hands cuffed behind their backs and shouting to be heard.

"It's all the same story," the uniformed Army officer said to Bao. "They're all rich. Their fathers will bail them out. It's all a big mistake."

"We'll see how big a mistake it is." Boa raised his bull horn to his mouth. "Let's get them checked in."

Officers shoved and cajoled people into lines in front of two folding tables. Behind the tables were uniformed policewomen with piles of forms. As each prisoner approached the front of the line, the women took their names, fingerprinted them, and collected their ID papers.

The papers were thrown carelessly into a plastic bin.

When the prisoners were processed and blood drawn, the uniformed officers herded them into a gymnasium. They sat on the bleachers or wandered around. Everywhere people wanted to know what was going on, why they were arrested.

When the gym was full, Colonel Bao entered, followed by his entourage.

"You are here," he said into his bull-horn, "because you have broken the law. You were frequenting a known drug source. Many of you used the drugs, many didn't.

"It doesn't matter. The mere fact that you were there makes you guilty. In case you don't know, use of or proximity to illegal drugs is a major offense. You will not go to trial. The fact that we apprehended you on those premises proves your guilt. You will be taken to work camps for two years to be rehabilitated."

Hoa gasped. She would have fallen to the floor if Ngoc hadn't caught her. Many others did fall.

"The buses are lined up outside," Bao said. "I expect that you will proceed in an orderly fashion. There will be no mercy for laggards."

The police shoved and poked the prisoners into lines.

Hoa and Ngoc clung to each other to keep from being separated.

"My father will find out about this," Ngoc said. "He will have us out of here in no time."

"Move it." A fat policeman shoved Ngoc with his night-stick. "I said move."

The lovers climbed the steps to the bus.

Ngoc stopped at the driver. "There's been a mistake. We shouldn't be here."

The driver spat at him. "Keep moving. Get a seat."

The people boarding shoved and pushed until Ngoc and Hoa were at the back of the bus. With no seats left, Hoa and Ngoc clung to straps.

The bus bumped and gyrated over the poorly maintained road all through the night. By morning, there was no sign that they had ever been in Hanoi.

The buses pulled through guarded gates at the work camp. It looked more like a prison. Gray factory buildings rose three stories above the parking lot. To the side were long white barracks. In front of the factory buildings was an administrative office building.

Hoa and Ngoc were herded into a line to the office building. The six hundred prisoners snaked way down the parking lot.

"Ngoc, my legs are on fire," Hoa said. "I can hardly walk."

"Shut up, you two." A uniformed guard shoved Hoa with his night-stick.

When their turn came, Hoa and Ngoc clung together as they were led into a small room. The room was white with a stainless steel table in the center of the room. A counter with cabinets below it and cabinets above filled one wall.

Two male guards stood beside the table.

"Strip."

"What? Huh?" Ngoc couldn't quite comprehend what they were saying.

One of the guards grabbed Hoa and yelled, "Strip," into her face.

She looked at Ngoc.

He shrugged.

The guard spun her around and unzipped the remains of her dress. "I said strip."

THE GUARDS USHERED Hoa to the women's group. Ngoc went with the men.

"I am Colonel Bao. You have been assigned to my factory to rehabilitate your worthless lives." Bao slapped his thigh for emphasis. "You will work here. You will do the job you are assigned, and you will not complain. We take dissidents very seriously."

Bao strutted back and forth at the front of the room. "You will be trained on your job by an experienced prisoner, then you will be expected to meet your production quotas. If you fail, you will be punished severely. Do you all understand?" He stopped and glared at the crowd of prisoners.

Ngoc looked about him. Nearly three hundred other men cowered in fear. These were doctors, lawyers, stockbrokers, rich men. Powerful men. And they were reduced to this.

"This is Captain Khang. He is the administrator of this facility. You will follow his orders explicitly. Remember, he possesses the power of life and death over you."

Khang stepped forward. A small man, even for a Vietnamese, he had a fierce grin on his face. "Welcome to Factory Thirty-One. You will produce sneakers and flip-flops for third world countries. Your work will be good, and you will meet your quotas. I cannot emphasize this enough. Those who do not meet their quotas are not worth the food or space they take up. It will be withheld until you are back on track."

After a long lecture on the do's and don'ts of the camp, guards herded Ngoc and the other men to the factory floor. There they were split up and assigned to work groups. Assembling flip-flops would occupy Ngoc's every waking hour for the rest of his life. Very few prisoners ever left the factory.

COLONEL BAO — HANOI

The raid was a great success. Colonel Bao hummed as he walked in from the parking lot. He had six hundred new workers for his shoe factory and the publicity exploded across the country, painting him as a hero. Better yet, the raid would help push another competitor out of business.

Bao entered his office to find a pot of tea and a handleless ceramic cup on the right side of his desk, as it was every day.

"Good morning, sir," his aide, standing by the desk, said. "I have today's reports for you." He set a pile of file folders on the desk.

"Very good, Thu. I'll look at them presently." He sat in his black leather chair. "Get me the file on the Americans."

"Yes, sir."

Thu, a thin man with huge, black-framed glasses hustled out of the room.

Bao poured himself a cup of tea. *Hmmm—there's something wrong here. I can smell it. Those Americans are not here as tourists.*

He pressed the button on his intercom. "Thu, have we gotten the intelligence report on those Americans yet?"

"Yes, sir," the electronic voice replied. "I'm incorporating it into the file now. I'll have it in a minute."

Good. They're spies. I know it.

Thu returned to the office and handed Bao a thick file folder. "Here's everything we have on them so far."

"Hmmm—" Bao opened the file. On the top, a picture of a young Mexican man stared up at him. He folded back the picture. He didn't look like the man Bao met at customs. His face was clear, not all scarred up. "Hi-gow-wa? Why does that name feel so familiar?" He scanned the file. "Came from a poor home, by American standards. Went to college. Played American football. Worked his way up to own his investigation firm. It all looks very average." He put the file down. "So why does it bother me so much?"

"Keep looking, sir. Intelligence doesn't have much on him. They've contacted a company in America that does background checks. We should have them for all four of the Americans by tomorrow."

"Okay, two men and two women. If they're spies, what could they be after?" Bao swallowed his last sip of tea. "Hi-gow-wa's a cybersecurity expert. Are they trying to spy on our systems?"

Thu shuffled his feet. "I don't know, sir. Couldn't he do that from home? I mean, with the Internet, anyone can go anywhere at any time."

"Hmm—" Bao tapped his pen on the desk. "I know I've heard of him. The others, no. We need to keep an eye on them. Put a security detail on all of them."

BAO PULLED a burner phone from one of the files in his lower desk drawer. He found the number and tapped it.

The phone rang four times, and he heard a voice.

"Sí, que quiere?"

"Gomez, this is Bao." English was their common language.

"Oh, *Sí, mi Coronel*. How may I help you today?" Gomez had a pronounced Mexican accent.

Bao paced back and forth behind his desk. "I have a problem. I have a tourist here in Vietnam. His name is Hi-gow-wa, Ted Hi-gow-wa, I can't place him. I know I know him, but I don't know where from. Since his name is Mexican, I thought I'd try you."

There was a pause on the line as if Gomez were accessing his personal hard drive.

"Hi-gow-wa? That doesn't sound Mexican." There was a slight pause. "Can you spell it for me?"

"H I G U E R A."

"Ah, *Sí,* Higuera. I remember him. He is the one who brought down El Pozolero. He and his girlfriend, La Reina.

Colonel Bao slammed his fist into a stack of file folders on his desk. "El Pozolero. Of course. That bastard cost me millions of dollars in lost revenue."

"He did worse than that. With the death of El Pozolero, he plunged *Mejico* into a drug war. When El Pozolero was *jefe*, there was peace among the cartels. No one dared challenge him. With him gone, all the cartels are fighting to take over his role."

Bao froze. "He almost ruined me. He must not leave Vietnam. What's the situation now?"

Gomez replied, "His girlfriend, La Reina, is the most powerful drug lord in the country, but she's always being challenged by others. They don't think a woman should run the country. I expect this war to go on until either she is dead, or all the others are. So far, I would say she's winning."

"Damn her, and damn Hi-gow-wa. She is not friendly to us. Can you keep taking your products from me in this chaos?"

Gomez was silent for a long moment. "I don't know—I will try. As long as your shipments are discreet, she won't notice them. But if she finds out how much money we are making, she might want to horn in."

"They must be stopped."

19

THE SECRET POLICE — HANOI

"Hi, everyone," Huong said as Ted's posse emerged from the elevator. She gave Kathy a big hug.

"Are you ready for a little skull-duggery?" Ted asked.

Huong smiled. "I've always been a bad girl." Ted noticed a small confrontation at the door.

"There he is again," Hope said. "The man in the raincoat."

Ted led them out of the hotel. Sure enough, the man in the raincoat followed at a safe distance.

"I've seen that Toyota before," Chris said, tilting his head forward. "They're tailing us."

"Oh, shit." Ted closed his eyes and shook his head. "We have to lose 'em. We need to meet with your dad," he said to Kathy.

"We can lose them in a crowded place," Kathy said.

Ted stepped to the curb and flagged down a taxi. The group crowded in.

"Where to?" the driver said in badly accented English.

"What's your most popular night club?" Ted asked.

"Fallen Moon," Huong said. "It always has the biggest crowd."

"Okay, let's go there."

"How are we going to lose them there?" Hope asked.

Ted raised his finger to his lips and shushed her.

"He might be secret police," Ted mouthed and pointed to the driver.

Hope nodded and looked at Chris and Kathy.

They nodded.

The cab ride was a kamikaze mission through the busiest part of Hanoi. By the time they arrived at the Fallen Moon, all five passengers were ready to fall on their knees and kiss the Earth.

A long line wrapped around the block. Two husky doormen controlled the flow into the club.

"Let me," Huong said. "Follow my lead."

She pulled the front of her dress down as far as it would go then walked up to the first doorman and asked him, in Vietnamese, "How long is the wait?"

He looked her over from head to foot before he replied.

"Maybe two hour."

"Oh, we can't wait that long," she said in her most seductive voice. "I have friends from America with me. I promised to show them Fallen Moon."

"Two hour."

"Maybe I'll call my uncle while we're waiting. You've heard of him surely. Colonel Bao." Huong let that hang in the air.

"Colonel Bao?"

"Yes. You know, the man that just shut down the New Century. I'm sure he wouldn't mind coming down to keep me company."

Huong's glare skewered the doorman. Ted could see his stolid resolve melting.

"If she can get us in here, we win," Hope said. "Our tail can't follow us in. He'll have to wait in line."

Chris shook his head. "Don't be too sure. If he flashes his badge, they'll let him right in."

"Okay, here's the plan," Ted whispered. "We get inside, then split up." He nodded toward Chris. "You, Huong, and Hope head to the bar. Kathy and I will look for a way out. You guys get a drink, mingle on the dance floor, keep them entertained. Kathy and I'll sneak out and go find her father."

"Come on, guys." Huong waved to them. "We're in."

"What did you have to promise him?" Kathy asked.

"Oh, I just said that Kathy and Hope would give him a three-way."

Hope's mouth fell open and she stared. Kathy knew better."

"I just sort of mentioned that my uncle was Head of Security for the whole country," Huong said. "The last thing they want is for any authorities to look too closely at them." She grinned a Cheshire Cat grin.

Her uncle's Head of Security? Ted scratched his head. *Could that be the same pendejo who interviewed me?*

Huong and the four Americans entered the bar to a chorus of boos and cat calls from the people waiting in line.

The bar was Western modern. Huge glass chandeliers hung from the two-story-high ceiling. They flashed and changed colors in time to the music. Spotlights passed over the crowd.

Deafening acid rock blasted from twelve-foot-tall speakers.

Three mirrored walls gave the room the impression of being much larger than it was. Crowds of young people in the latest Western fashions did the bump and grind on the dance floor.

"I feel kinda out of place," Kathy said as she pulled at her conservative blue dress that came down to her knees, by far the longest dress in the establishment. "If I knew we were coming here, I could have dressed more appropriately."

Ted, in black jeans, a white body-hugging turtleneck, and a black blazer fit right in.

Hope with a white blouse and short blue skirt was less conservative than Kathy, but still stood out in the crowd. Her body type was all but unknown in the Far East.

"Not to worry, chica," Hope said. "You guys are getting out of here before anyone has a chance to notice you anyway."

Ted noticed a small confrontation at the door. Their tail was trying to force his way in. The doormen blocked him. The tail pulled out a wallet and shouted at the doormen.

Chris slipped his arm around Hope's waist. Or, actually, around her rib cage since his arms weren't long enough to reach all the way down to her waist. "Let's hit the bar." He turned to Ted. "You guys better find your way out."

"Let's go." Ted took Kathy's arm. "There must be a back door."

"Let's try the service entrance. It must be through the kitchen."

She led him toward heavy swinging doors with windows in them. "I worked for a catering company during school. I know my way around clubs and hotels."

They passed through the doors into a service area. Servers and busboys hustled about taking care of business.

Past the service area, a large stainless steel kitchen bustled. Cooks and chefs in white with black skull caps shouted and moved rapidly at their stations.

"This way." Kathy took Ted's hand. His heart rate sped up. She led him to the back of the kitchen. Through a door, they found themselves in a hallway. To the left, it led to what looked like offices. To the right was a loading area for big trucks.

Kathy led him right. "There must be a way out here."

The loading dock was at least four feet off the ground. Next to it was a set of steps.

They hustled down the steps into a dirty alley. "Okay, let's see if it's clear in the street," Ted said.

"No, they might still be watching the streets. Let's go through that building." Kathy pointed to the building across the alley with its own loading dock.

They climbed the stairs to the dock, which had a rolling steel door at its back edge.

"We can't get through there," Ted said.

"Try this door; see if it's open." Kathy indicated the human-sized door next to the rolling door.

Ted tried the handle. "Locked."

"Damn."

"Not to worry." Ted reached into his inner jacket pocket and pulled out a set of lock picks. "Catrina taught me well."

He went to work on the door and unlocked it in thirty seconds. "C'mon." He held the door open for Kathy.

They were inside a huge fish market. Stalls went off into the distance. The air smelled of three-day-old fish.

Incandescent bulbs in fixtures that looked like China caps hung from wires from the high ceiling. Every other light was left on to provide enough illumination to get around.

"Where's the front door?" Kathy asked.

"Up there, I would think."

Ted and Kathy made their way past the stalls to a huge rolling door. Next to it was a person-sized door.

They had no problem with the lock. They were on the inside. Ted unlocked the door, and they stepped out into the street.

"I THINK we've decoyed them enough," Chris said, almost out of breath from dancing.

"Oh, this is fun." Hope flashed him a huge smile. "Can't we stay a little longer?"

"I think we should get back to the hotel. Ted might need us."

"Spoil sport." Hope flashed him a pout, turned, and left the dance floor. Huong danced with an attractive Vietnamese man. Hope tapped her on the shoulder as she passed by.

There at the bar, right where they left him, the man in the raincoat nursed a drink. They made sure to walk past him on the way to their table.

They collected their gear and headed for the front door. Chris looked over his shoulder to see the raincoat man talking into a handheld radio.

"This stinks." Chris pulled on his coat. "I feel like human bait."

"We're doing this for Teddy. We'll be all right." Hope followed Chris out the door. They joined hands and strolled down the sidewalk. Huong trailed them like a third wheel.

Shortly, the raincoat man appeared behind them.

As they passed, the gray Toyota pulled away from the curb.

The car slowly drove past them, then jumped the curb and stopped in front of them, blocking their way.

Chris turned to run, but the raincoat man stood before him, with a nasty looking pistol in his hand.

"You will turn and put your hands on the roof of the car," Raincoat said in badly accented English.

"What? Why? What have we done?"

"No questions. Now turn." He grabbed Hope's arm and tried to turn her.

She spun out of his grasp and planted a kick square in his chest. He went stumbling backward and fell on his butt.

"Run!" she shouted as she stumbled in her high heels.

With Chris's long legs, he quickly caught up with her. Huong was surprisingly fast for such a small person. Chris heard the Toyota start up and pull off the curb.

"We need to get off the road." Chris gasped for breath.

As they passed a corner, he saw a park. "Here, let's go in there."

Hope and Huong followed as they left the road and sprinted across green lawn. They stopped for a second and the women kicked off their heels.

The Toyota jumped the curb and pursued them over the grass.

Chris, Huong, and Hope dodged around a public rest room, then ran toward a wooded area.

Sirens filled the air and lights flashed everywhere. A flood of policemen swarmed out of the wooded area.

Chris stopped in his tracks. "Stop. There's no use. We'll never evade all of them." He put his hands in the air.

Hope stamped her foot on the ground. "Damn, we almost made it."

The uniformed officers were much faster and more wary than the secret policeman. They slapped cuffs on all three parties and shoved them into the backs of separate patrol cars.

"WHAT THE FUCK are you doing hanging out with those spies?" Colonel Bao wiped his red brow. He fought to control his breathing. "What were you thinking?" he shouted into the telephone.

"They're not spies. They're my friends." Huong's voice was shaky but defiant.

Bao stared into the phone for a moment. "Your FRIENDS? They can't be your friends. They're foreigners, Americans. They're using you."

"Uncle, Kathy was my roommate in college. She's my best friend."

"You better find a new best friend. I don't think she's going anywhere."

"You stop that. You can't bully me."

Bao paused and thought. "Maybe we can save something from this situation." He rubbed at the tick on his chin. "I want you to spend a lot of time with them. They trust you. Find out why they are in Vietnam for me."

"No!" Huong shouted through the phone line. "I won't spy for you. They're just normal tourists. You have no reason to suspect them of anything."

"I suspect them of everything. We have a file on Hi-gow-wa. He's known to our secret police."

"I don't believe you."

"Well, you better. I love you like my own child, but there could be dire consequences when we find out what they're up to. I don't know if even I could save you." He slammed down the phone. "Damn her and her fucking mother. My brother let her be too indulgent with that brat."

20

ESCAPE AND INTERROGATION — HANOI

Ted and Kathy stuck to the shadows as they made their way out of the center of town.

"Can we catch a cab?" Kathy asked breathlessly.

"I don't think we should. You never know who reports to the secret police."

"Well, my feet hurt."

Ted stopped to admire her shapely legs. "Take off those heels."

Kathy harrumphed as she slid her shoes off. "These are Jimmy Choo. If something happens to them, I'll never forgive you."

The pair moved silently toward the older part of town. Traffic and crowds disappeared. High-rises gave way to one-story shops and dwellings. Carefully maintained sidewalks gave way to dirt paths along the road. Open drainage ditches smelled like sewers.

"Youch." Kathy jumped as she stepped on something sharp. "Damn." She hobbled around on one foot as she dug out a piece of glass. "They need to keep their streets clean."

Ted handed her his handkerchief. "Here, clean up that blood."

She looked at the handkerchief.

"It's clean," Ted said. "Where's your dad staying?"

"With his cousin. It can't be too far now." Kathy led the way after daubing her foot.

After several more blocks Kathy said, "There it is. The green house."

They knocked at the door and an older Vietnamese man opened it a crack.

"Hi, we're looking for Chun," Kathy said in Vietnamese.

The man smiled and opened the door. "Hein, how good to see you," the man replied, using Kathy's Vietnamese name.

"What's he saying?" Ted asked.

"He's welcoming us."

"Please come in." The old man made a welcoming gesture with his hand.

The home was neat and clean. A Vietnamese woman came racing from the kitchen with a teapot in her hand.

Kathy gestured toward the couple. "This is my Uncle Chi and my Aunt An." She turned to the people and said something in Vietnamese. "I just introduced you to them. You should shake hands and bow slightly."

Ted did as instructed. Chi put his left hand on top of Ted's hand and gave a nod.

Kathy followed Ted into the room.

"Papa," Kathy shouted and ran to embrace Chun.

"My baby," he said in English and kissed the top of her head. "How have you made out in the big city?"

Kathy kneeled on the floor next to the table An had set with the tea and cookies. "Not so well. We got our gear delivered to the hotel room, but the secret police are following us."

"What? You didn't lead them here . . . "

"Don't worry about it, Mr. Nguyen," Ted said. "We shook them off at a nightclub. We weren't followed."

Chun joined Kathy and his cousins at the table. An poured five cups of tea.

"You can't be too careful in this country," Chun said. "Everyone is an informant. Trust no one."

Ted sat on the floor and joined the others. "We're strangers in a strange land. We're depending on you to keep us safe."

Chun pointed to a stack of aluminum cases at the back of the room. "We removed your gear from your hotel room. You'll leave from here." He reached inside his shirt and produced a map on flimsy paper. "This is a map of where you're going." He handed it to Ted.

The paper felt thin in Ted's hand. "This is—"

"Flash paper," Chun said. "Touch a match to it and it goes up in less than a second."

Ted rubbed the map in his fingers.

"Do you have a lighter?" Chun asked.

Ted looked at Kathy. She shook her head. "No . . . uh, none of us smoke."

"Here." Chun handed Ted a Bic lighter. "We leave tomorrow."

THE CHINESE ARMY truck bounced over the pot-holed road. They had been on the road for hours. The guard sitting up front nodded and closed his eyes. The driver fought to keep control of the vehicle. Every couple of minutes he swerved to the side of the road and had to veer back. The three men in the back were no more alert.

By the time they knew there was a problem, it was too late. The IED exploded, blowing the truck off the road and rolling it onto its side. The driver and guard were killed instantaneously, necks snapped by the violent explosion. The three men in the back were battered but alive. They stumbled to regain their balance, grabbed their weapons, and spilled out of the back of the truck in a chaos of confusion.

They were cut down by automatic gunfire as they stood dazed.

Six men in combat fatigues and black masks emerged from the bushes. They checked the bodies and removed their weapons.

"Okay, let's get this mess unloaded," the leader shouted.

A panel truck pulled out of a side road covered in jungle growth and drove to the back of the ruined vehicle. The six men climbed into the truck and started shifting its cargo to the panel truck.

"The boss is going to be happy about this," a short, masked man said.

"He's bat-shit crazy. He just declared war on Colonel Bao. Bao has the entire Army at his disposal." The leader shoved the other man in the shoulder. "We'll be lucky to live to see Sunday."

"But if we succeed," the first man said, "We'll control the drug trade throughout Vietnam."

COLONEL BAO'S magnificent home sat in an exclusive district in Hanoi. Huong grew up there and often hung out there when she wanted to be alone. Almost always empty, except for Bao's wife, Aunt Bie, it gave Huong the freedom of the place.

Huong walked down the long hall. Her uncle's office was locked. She rattled the door, then knocked. As usual, her uncle was not there. *Does he ever come home?*

Moving down the hall, Huong came to the billiards room. She stood in the doorway and took in the opulence. With red walls and gold trim, a huge, high-end pool table dominated the room. She slipped inside.

A golden Buddha mounted on a small throne and silk throw sat at one end of the room. She rubbed his belly for good luck, wandered over to the pool table, and racked up the balls. She found a cue to her liking and chalked the end. She loved the smell of the chalk and the scrunching sound of tip meeting the chalk.

Centering the white cue ball, she took a mighty shot. A loud pop and the triangle of balls exploded. The green felt was covered with balls.

Easy pickin's. She lined up her first shot. She gently hit the ball and listened to the satisfying clack as ball met ball. The fifteen ball slowly rolled toward the side pocket, then dropped in.

Good work, girl. She lined up her next shot.

From down the hall came the clamor of male voices.

Oh shit. Uncle Bao. She quickly racked her cue and looked for a place to hide. Bao did not approve of women playing pool, smoking, or having any other kind of fun. He most especially wouldn't approve of her short skirt and tank top.

The cabinet under the bar was empty so Huong dove in.

"Come, gentlemen, let me pour you a drink." Bao walked over to the bar and pulled down four glasses.

Huong heard the tinkle of glassware and the swoosh of liquid pouring.

"This is a Rémy Martin Louis XIII. I think you will enjoy it," Bao said.

There was a grumbling of ascent.

"Let's get down to business, shall we?"

Huong didn't recognize the voice.

"That is why I brought you here." Bao's voice sounded irritated. "We have a problem with a spy called Hi-gow-wa."

"I don't care about spies," a high-pitched voice squeaked. "I'm concerned with our shipment being hijacked. You are supposed to control all drug shipments in Vietnam."

"They are one and the same problem, Vinh," Colonel Bao said. "I know this Hi-gow-wa is a spy. I know he has links to the Baja Cartel. He must be here in their interest. No one would have the balls to hijack one of our shipments, then Hi-gow-wa appears and we lost a shipment. What does that tell you?"

"If he is involved in this, he must not be allowed to roam free." This from a gravelly voice.

A chorus of voices followed.

"We must stop him."

"He must not be allowed to leave Vietnam."

"I think it would be best for all concerned," Bao said, "if he just disappeared."

THE GUARDS HERDED Chris to an interview room. He looked at himself in the two-way mirror. His long, blond hair was a rat's nest and his clothes rumpled and stained. He had no idea what happened to the women.

He was led into the room and handcuffed to a table. He sat at the table for over an hour until the door opened and a man in full uniform walked in. The man had a file folder in his hand.

"Hmmm — Christopher Hardwick," he said. "I am Colonel Bao, Head of Security for the state of Vietnam."

He paused to let that sink in.

If he's looking for me to quake, he's going to be disappointed. Chris leaned back in his chair. "Why am I here?"

Bao walked around the table, taking in Chris from all angles. "Oh, I think you know, Mr. Hardwick." He came back around the table and sat down in a chair opposite Chris. He opened his file folder and laid it on the table.

Chris could see his picture, but the rest of the paper was covered in Vietnamese characters.

Colonel Bao stared at him, and Chris stared back. No word was exchanged for the longest time.

"You have gotten yourself in a bit of trouble, Mr. Hardwick." The colonel closed the folder and tapped on it.

"Oh, c'mon, Bao." Chris smirked at him. "I'm a defense attorney. I've been interrogated by experts. You don't think your little performance will rattle me, do you?

Bao slammed his hands down on the table. "You take this lightly, do you?" he shouted. "Be cavalier. You will spend the rest of your life in Vietnam." His voice softened. "Unless −"

Chris gave him a bored look.

"— Unless you tell me what I want to know."

"And that would be —?"

Bao put both hands on the table and leaned over close to Chris. "What is Hi-gow-wa doing in Vietnam? Why have you come here?"

Bao's breath smacked of onions and garlic. Chris smiled. "You think you frighten me? He sat back in his chair. "For your information, we are here merely as tourists. Kathy wanted to show Ted her heritage. I expect that when we get back, Ted'll want to take her to Mexico."

"You — are — lying." Bao's face turned red. "You will remain my prisoner until you tell me what I want to know. Prepare yourself for a very long incarceration."

AFTER A PRE-DAWN WAKEUP call and a long, hard drive to nowhere in the back of an old, beat-up Toyota pickup, Ted, Kathy, and Chun spent the rest of the day laboring through the forest. The sun was low under the jungle canopy. Ted paced the clearing. Chun sat on a log in a trance-like state, and Kathy wandered through the trees.

Time stopped. Ted had no idea how long they'd been waiting in the clearing, but it felt like an eternity.

As darkness slowly spread through the trees, Ted heard voices. A high-pitched, almost bird-like, conversation grew louder.

Chun sprang to his feet. He stood in front of two ancient Vietnamese. "My father," he said in Vietnamese. "I am so glad to see you." He clasped his hands together and nodded to his father.

"That's my grandpa," Kathy whispered to Ted.

"Come," the elder Mr. Nguyen said. "We have a camp set up close to here."

Ted, Kathy, and Chun followed the two old men at a respectful distance.

"Where's he taking us?" Kathy asked her father in English.

"To a safe place where we can discuss our plans."

"Plans?" Kathy scoffed. "As far as I can tell, there aren't any plans."

It was long dark before the travelers reached their destination.

The camp was built on a rising hillside. Two large boulders framed the entrance to a cave. A cheery fire roared in front of the cave.

"I want you to meet two of my friends," Grandpa said in Vietnamese. Chun translated. "This is Han and this is Duc." The two men bowed. "We all worked together on the Underground Railroad when we were young."

"We used this spot as one of the waypoints on our Underground Railroad," Duc said.

"We are honored to be in this place." Kathy put her hands together and bowed slightly.

"What's going on?" Ted asked.

"They're just welcoming us to their camp. They say they used it for the Underground Railroad."

Ted's eyes bounced from speaker to speaker as if he were Huong blew past the front desk, watching a tennis match. He understood nothing of what was being said.

Finally, after an extended conversation, Chun turned to Ted. "They say they have heard from Roc tribesmen of rumors of a POW camp. They say it is supposed to be in the Quang Binh Province, far to the north and east of here."

"How far?"

"Far. We cannot reach it by car. It will take several day's journey on foot."

"Crap. Why can't anything be easy?"

Chun looked down and pawed at the ground with his feet.

"That's not the worst. It's in an off-limits area. No one is allowed there."

"Of course not."

Duc produced an ancient scroll from inside his robe. He said something and handed it to Chun.

Chun accepted the scroll and bowed to Duc, then to his father. "This is a map. It will get us in the general area."

"What do you mean, 'us', Dad." Kathy spoke in a low voice. "You're not going any further. You're getting too old for these kinds of shenanigans."

"You will need a guide. Someone to interpret for you."

Kathy shook her head. "What am I? Chopped liver?"

Chun looked pleadingly at his daughter. "No. You must remain in Hanoi. This is no job for a woman."

"You can't be serious." Kathy laughed. "Join us in the twenty-first century, Dad. Women can do anything they want."

"But you are my daughter. My precious. I cannot risk you."

"Dad, it's a done deal. I go where Ted goes."

What? Ted spun his head around. *Did I hear that right or was I just imagining?*

"We'll head back to Hanoi in the morning and meet up with Chris and Hope. We'll get our gear and head to Quang Binh." The Dragon Lady left no room for dissent.

21

THE PLAN — HANOI

Huong stormed up the steps to the police station like a doughboy going over the top of the trenches in World War I. Desperately trying to keep up with her rapid footsteps, her lawyer, a middle-aged man in an expensive suit, followed.

Huong blew past the front desk, blasted through a door, and rushed down a hallway to the chief's office.

"What is the meaning of this?" she demanded as she stormed into the office.

"Huh —?" The chief looked up from his paperwork. He took in Huong in all her righteous indignation. "What are you talking about? Who are you? How did you get in here?"

The lawyer motioned Huong toward a chair.

"I'm Bao Huong. My uncle is Colonel Bao Van Doc, and I'm outraged that you have imprisoned my friend."

The chief fumbled with his glasses and picked up a folder off his desk. "Hold on. Wait a minute. What are you talking about?"

Huong closed her eyes, exhaled a long breath, and glared into the chief's eyes. "My friend. Christopher Hardwick. The tall, blond American. You have him in jail here. What are the charges?"

Understanding flashed across the chief's face. "Hardwick. Yes. He is here at Colonel Bao's request."

"No. You must have misunderstood my uncle's request. He wants him released immediately and offered your formal apologies."

The chief laughed. "I don't know what you are playing at girl, but orders are orders."

Huong turned to her long-suffering lawyer who had not yet had the chance to utter a word. "Mr. Dinh, please show the chief the letter."

Dinh set his alligator skin briefcase on his lap and opened it. He pulled out a file folder and took a sheet of paper out. "Here." He offered the paper to the chief.

"What is this?" the chief asked. He took a moment to read the letter. His eyes bulged. "No, this can't be. Bao was here himself."

"Yes, and as you see, he admits he made a mistake, and that the prisoner should be released — immediately."

Huong smiled to herself. She couldn't be prouder. She started forging her uncle's signature when she was in grade school. By now, she was an expert, she even knew which seals and ribbons to attach to a document.

"I – I ah – I am sorry for the misunderstanding, Ms. Nguyen." He pushed a button on his intercom. "Have the American released immediately." He turned to Huong. "It will take a little while to process all the paperwork."

"Well, do it quickly." Her Imperial Majesty stood and walked out of the office, leaving her lawyer huffing behind her.

RETURNING TO HANOI, Chun, Ted, and Kathy found Chun's cousin's green house. All were exhausted and fell into deep sleep on the bamboo flooring.

The next morning, as they sipped their tea, Chi brought a well-dressed man into the room.

"This is Giang," Chun said. "He and his friends know everything going on in Vietnam."

Ted and Kathy bowed to Giang, and Kathy said something in Vietnamese.

"While we were away," Chun said, "they were looking for a location for the POW camp."

Giang bowed. "I think we may have found something."

"You speak English very well," Ted said.

Giang smiled and nodded. "I went to school at Cornell in New York State."

"What have you learned?" Kathy asked.

"Let me see your map." Giang put a hand out.

Kathy reached into her purse and produced the document.

Giang spread the map out on the table. "Hmm — I see. Yes, this map is good. It shows the right area." He pulled a pen from his pocket and pointed. "Here, or here, or here." He noted three locations. It could be at any of those points, but your friends are right. It must be in this area."

"Wow. That narrows it down a lot, but we still have three locations to search," Chun said.

"Maybe not." Ted flipped back the comma of black hair that always fell over his left eye. "Before we left, my friend and I hacked into the DOD network. We found a surveillance satellite over the area"

"You what?" Kathy nearly jumped up off the floor. "Ted, that's illegal. It's national security. You could spend the rest of your life in Guantanamo."

"Don't worry. I've sparred with these dudes before. Chris knows how to handle them."

She just shook her head.

Hmm—I wonder if this is going to be a problem between us, if there is an us. She's such a goody two-shoes. He scratched his head. *A decade ago, I would have agreed with her. Have I changed that much?*

"Anyway, we found what could be a prison camp about here." He indicated the first location. "We'll go there first."

"Very good." Giang nodded. "That would be my choice as well." He sipped his tea. "There is supposed to be only one prisoner there. An American."

Ted gasped. *Could it really be true? Is it Uncle Gino?*

"How do we get there?" Kathy pulled out her cell phone and brought up her note app.

"It is a long journey. We have arranged it. You must not let the secret police follow you. Anyone caught in the area will be shot on sight." He stopped to let that sink in. "All supplies and staff are brought into the compound by helicopter. It will take three days to hike in after the road runs out."

"Why the secrecy? Why the security? What are they hiding after all these years?" Ted put down his cup and looked into Giang's eyes.

"All we know is that this area was secured long ago," Giang said. "After the war."

This smells to high Heaven. Ted replied, "Go on."

"We secured your transportation to the trail head. From there you are on your own."

"Got it," Ted said with a firm nod.

"There is one other item of importance." Giang paused to get their attention. "The secret police are executing a nationwide manhunt for you. Colonel Bao is furious Chris escaped. He'll stop at nothing to find you. You cannot go back to your hotel."

"Shit." Ted clinched his fist and pulled it to his chest.

"We have secured your luggage." Giang rook a pack of cigarettes from his pocket. "It will be brought here in the morning.

Kathy pointed to the back of the room. "Most of what we need is in those aluminum cases anyway. We're not tourists from this point out."

"Where are your friends, anyway?" Giang asked.

"Hell, if I know." Ted turned to Kathy. "Kathy?"

"I'll call Huong and have them meet us here."

HOPE LEANED against the wall with her arms folded over her chest as she watched Huong pace furiously back and forth in front of the steps to the police station.

"They said he would be released immediately," Huong growled. "What if something went wrong? Maybe they called my uncle."

"Easy, Chica." Hope reached out and grabbed Huong's hand. "We don't know anything yet. It may just take a long time to do the paperwork."

"But what if –"

"You're just buying trouble. Wait until something happens before you worry about it."

"Good afternoon, ladies –"

Hope looked up and saw her tall blond god coming down the steps with his long locks flying in the breeze.

Ted's right, they should have cast Chris to play Thor. "Chris," she yelled and ran to him. She put her arms around him, and he lifted her off the ground and twirled her around.

"—Miss me?"

She turned her face up to him and opened her mouth. He met her lips with a long, husky kiss.

"Hey, lovebirds," Huong cut in. "We better get out of here. There's no telling when my uncle's going to find out about this."

Hope let go of her squeeze and smiled at Huong. She was beginning to like the girl. The fact that Huong was shorter than Hope's diminutive five-foot-one frame might have had something to do with it. Hope had heard so many short jokes she didn't even notice them anymore.

That day none of it mattered. Everything was roses and lollipops. She hadn't been able to admit to even herself what would happen if they couldn't get Chris out of the pokey. Birds sang and puffy little clouds took on the shapes of ice cream castles in the air.

"I knew those bastards couldn't hold me." Chris blew on his knuckles and rubbed them against his shoulder. "I gave that son-of-a-bitch, Bao, more than he bargained for."

"Hold on there, cowboy." Hope slugged Chris in the shoulder. "You have Huong to thank for that. She got you out."

"Huh? What did she do?"

"Only committed a felony to spring you. She forged her uncle's signature on a document ordering your release."

"Holy crap." He turned to Huong. "Thank you." He took both of her hands in his and kissed her left hand.

Hope laughed at the shock on Huong's face.

"Yes, and we better get out of here before they figure out what I did." Huong broke away from Chris and started down the street.

"Where will we go?" Hope asked.

"We can't go back to our hotel." Chris glanced behind him. "They'll be looking for us."

"I know an underground nightclub we can go to," Huong took off down the street.

"And then what?" Hope ran to catch up.

"I don't know. Wait for Ted and Kathy to contact us, I guess."

BAO'S ANGER — HANOI

Bao sat at the desk in his home office, talking on the telephone.

"What about the other American?" a reedy voice asked.

"What other American?" Bao's patience waned.

"The big one. Hardwick."

Bao furrowed his brow. "Hardwick? He's in the city jail. I will deal with him as time permits."

"I thought you knew everything," the voice mocked. "He was released today."

"What – How?"

"Your niece brought a letter from you to the chief requiring that he be released immediately."

"No." Bao slammed his hand on his desk. "It can't be," he shouted. "I never signed such a letter."

"Be that as it may, Hardwick has disappeared."

BAO STORMED into the police chief's office. "How could you let him go?"

The chief looked up, saw who was yelling at him, and jumped to his feet, scattering paperwork in all directions. "Let who go, Colonel Bao?"

"The American." Bao slammed the glass door behind him, and pictures shook on the walls. "Hardwick. I gave specific orders that he was not to be released."

"But – but – you sent a letter ordering him to be released."

"What?" Bao kicked a chair over. "I did no such thing."

"Uh –" The chief's eyes grew wide. "I have the letter. Your niece and her lawyer delivered it for you."

Bao grabbed the chief by the collar. "I signed no such piece of paper. Let me see it."

The chief pushed a button on his intercom. "Ping, bring me the Hardwick file."

Moments later a uniformed officer handed the chief a manila folder.

The chief leafed through the folder and produced a document. "Here it is, sir. That is your signature is it not?"

Bao grabbed the letter. "No! I never saw this." He stared at his signature. "It's a forgery." That was his signature. *How could it have gotten there?* "I did not authorize his release."

"But, sir, your niece was insistent. She said you made a mistake and were very sorry."

"A MISTAKE?" Bao grabbed a picture from the chief's desk and flung it across the room. "A mistake? I don't make mistakes. I never make mistakes." He took a few deep breaths and, by an incredible force of will, calmed himself. "Huong came to your office personally?"

"Yes, sir." The chief still stood at attention. "She and her lawyer. She was terribly angry. The document looked real."

"Huong? My niece came to get the American out?" His voice dropped. "That's not possible. That's an act of treason." Bao took a deep breath. "We must find the American. He's a spy. This is a matter of national security." He looked at the chief. "Do you have any idea where he went?"

"No, sir. The two women waited for him outside and they left together."

"Two women?"

"Yes, sir. Your niece and the Mexican girl."

"Start a search immediately." Bao's face was red and sweat poured down his forehead. "I want every restaurant, bar, hotel, and hostel searched. Put a hold on their passports. I don't want them leaving the country. Put out an APB. I want every policeman in the country looking for them."

"Yes, sir. What about the secret police, sir?"

"I control the VPS. What I do with them is my business."

Colonel Bao deflated.

The chief sat down behind his desk. He looked at the items swept onto the floor. "Yes, sir. We'll find them. Make no mistake about that."

"Where are the Mexican and the woman? We need to round up all of them."

"MEET us at Uncle Chi's house," Kathy said into her cell phone.

"All right," Huong replied. "Give me the address again."

Kathy repeated the address. "And be careful. They're looking for us."

"No worries. We won't take public transportation. I have a friend with a car. He'll bring us over."

Half an hour later, Huong showed up at the green house with Chris and Hope in tow.

"Good. You made it." Ted held the door open for the three. "What happened? Where have you been?"

Chris related the story of his imprisonment and escape.

"Holy shit." Ted turned to Huong. "Are you going to be okay? I mean, won't your uncle be mad?"

Huong found herself a chair. "Oh, don't worry. I've done all sorts of stuff he's had to get me out of. He'll yell and scream and be mad for a day or two, then everything will go back to normal."

Ted smiled.

"I have something else to tell you." Huong burst with excitement. "I overheard a conversation between my uncle and some men I don't know. They're out to get you. They think you had something to do with a hijack."

"What?" Ted shook his head. "What hijack?"

"Apparently, someone intercepted one of my uncle's shipments and stole it."

"Oh, Christ," Chris said. "That's all we need. Now he's really motivated to find us." Chris turned to Ted. "So, have we got a plan?"

"Sit around the table." Ted spread out his map on the shiny teak table with short legs.

The others kneeled around the table. "Okay, this is where we enter the jungle. Giang will get us this far. Then we're on our own." He stopped to look at the others.

Chris pulled his lips tight and nodded. Hope looked at her brother with fierce eyes.

Ted went on to explain the plan. Chris and Hope added some ideas.

"We'll leave first thing in the morning," Ted said. "Giang has bus tickets for us."

"Let's check out our gear," Hope said. "We can't afford to make any mistakes out there."

Each of the team opened their aluminum cases and went over the contents. Survival gear, food, water, their CAT suits, and weapons.

"I don't like this," Kathy said, holding up her pistol by two fingers. "I told you we can't use guns in a foreign country. What if you shoot someone? There's no way our government is going to be able to get you out of a murder charge."

"Take a deep breath, Kathy," Chris said. "Ted and I discussed this. We'll load the firearms with tranquilizer darts. We're not going to kill anyone."

It was early morning before the four went to sleep.

THE BUSH — BACK COUNTRY VIETNAM

G iang showed up before daylight. After a quick breakfast, the four adventurers loaded their backpacks and set out with Giang.

They walked a few blocks to the bus station, where Giang already had their tickets.

"Take your direction from me," Giang told them. "When I get up, you get up. Follow me off the bus."

He boarded the bus with them but sat separately at the front of the bus.

"Not exactly first class," Ted remarked.

"Oh, knock it off." Hope poked him in the shoulder. "You've ridden on a lot worse in Mexico."

The bus pulled out. With nearly forty people on board, it reeked of humanity. It took the better part of an hour to work its way through well-maintained city streets. When it finally broke out into the country, well-tended fields surrounded the bumpy highway.

After two hours, the bus stopped in a small town. Giang got off, so the crew followed. The street was lined with wooden buildings, but Ted could see thatched-roof huts further out. The air smelled of wood smoke and animal dung.

"God, am I glad to get off that contraption," Hope said. "The ride is so bumpy I thought I give myself a black eye with my boobs."

"This is a biology break," Giang said, as he faced away from the Americans. "We still have more than an hour to go."

Ted and Chris followed the men into the bushes. Hope and Kathy trooped after the women in another direction, careful to not talk to any strangers. Anyone could be an informant. Just their presence on a bus could set off alarms.

They returned to the bus and as they walked up the aisle, every pair of eyes fastened on them. They settled down for the rest of the ride. Ted slumped in his seat and closed his eyes.

"How can he do that?" Kathy asked Hope. "How can he just sit there and sleep with all the tension going around."

"My brother can sleep anywhere, anytime." Hope smiled at Kathy. "If there was a Kentucky Derby for sleeping, I'd bet my whole wad on Ted."

As darkness descended onto the Vietnamese countryside, the bus pulled into another stop.

Giang got off and the Americans followed. He walked around behind the terminal building. "This is where I leave you," he said. He shook hands with each of the team. "May God go with you."

"What do we do next?" Chris asked.

"There is a car waiting for you." Giang pointed to an ancient red Toyota. "My cousin will take you the rest of the way."

The girls hugged him, and he disappeared into the depot.

The crew walked over to the waiting Toyota.

"Mr. Ted," a middle-aged Vietnamese man said in his native language. "Put your packs in the back."

Kathy translated as he got out of the car and opened the trunk.

They crowded into the car. It wasn't bad for Ted and the

women, but six-foot two-inch Chris had his knees up around his ears.

"Shit," Chris said. "This is like a clown car."

"Damn, I forgot to bring my red nose," Ted replied.

The ride wasn't long. They arrived at a trailhead shortly.

"This is where I leave you," the driver said in Vietnamese. "Giang says you know what to do from here."

Two trailbikes sat by the side of the road.

"You take these up the trail as far as you can go."

Kathy translated again.

"Gee," Hope said. "They really thought of everything."

"Like van Moltke said, 'no plan survives first contact with the enemy,'" Chris said.

Hope looked at him and shrugged.

"Let's saddle up," Ted said as he unloaded the backpacks from the trunk.

Each team member took their pack and headed to the motorbikes. They attached their packs to the rear fenders and climbed on board.

"Should we take our helmets out of our packs?" Kathy asked. No helmets came with the bikes.

"Might as well," Ted said. "We already stick out like sore thumbs here. I guess it doesn't matter if we look a little weird.

They dug into their packs and produced the gold Millennium Systems cybernetic helmets.

"Check this out," Ted said, turning his helmet invisible. He sat on the bike like the Headless Horseman.

"Get serious, *Hermano*," Hope said. "We all need to concentrate and be hyperalert from here on out."

Ted turned off the invisibility and started the bike. He looked at his map and said to Chris, "You got the map memorized, bro?"

"Got it." Chris said. They didn't really need the paper map from there on out. Chris's eidetic memory stored it in his brain. Whenever he needed it, he could call up an image of the map in his mind and zoom in if necessary. "No problem. Besides, if we need to, we can always call up a map on our helmets' heads-up displays."

"I'm glad these things work off satellites and not Wi-Fi," Kathy said. "There's no way we'd access the Internet way out here."

Kathy climbed on the bike behind Ted. Chris and Hope mounted up and the two couples headed into the jungle.

The warmth of the day became hot and moist as soon as they were under the canopy. Ted immediately soaked the armpits and back of his T-shirt with sweat. *Thank God we're moving fast enough to keep the bugs off.*

The trail twisted and turned through the jungle. At places they had to stop and lift the bikes over fallen logs. Ted reveled in the uneven trail and laughed as he flew over bumps. He felt Kathy clutching his waist ever tighter.

Ted raised his hand and stopped his bike. "I think we better stop here for the night. It's too dangerous to keep going on in the dark."

Hope and Kathy set up the tents. Ted found rocks to make a fire pit while Chris hunted down firewood.

Soon a comfortable blaze lit the campsite.

"What's for dinner?" Ted asked.

Hope pawed through her packets of freeze-dried food. "Let's see. You can have spaghetti and meatballs, beef stew, chicken noodle casserole, or pork chops."

They settled on the spaghetti, and Hope warmed the meal.

After dinner, Ted spread the sleeping bags out in their tent.

"You might want to zip them together," Chris said from his tent. "Two bodies in a bag will keep you warmer."

"I – uh – don't know. Kathy? – "

"Oh, don't be a prude." Kathy waved a hand at him. "Remember: we're big kids now."

They climbed in their bag and Ted turned his back to Kathy and slept on his side. *A little bit safer this way.*

He slipped off into a shallow sleep. Then he felt something around his waist.

Kathy spooned with him and had her arm around him.

Crap. Does she want to fool around?

"Uh, Miss Kathy, is that your arm around my waist?"

"Shut up and go to sleep. Enjoy."

BAO WAS FURIOUS. Huong had never seen him this mad.

"You betrayed your country." He paced around the billiard room as Huong sat in a carved chair. "This is nothing less than treason. Those people are spies."

"Uncle, don't be ridiculous. They're just kids on vacation."

Bao spun to look at Huong. "SHUT UP!" Spittle flew from his lips. "I know they are involved with the Baja Cartel in Mexico."

"No. That's not possible. I know these people."

"You know nothing." He leaned over Huong with a hand on each arm of the chair. "Where are they? Where are they going?"

Huong began to sweat. "I – I don't know."

Bao slapped her across the face. "You're lying to me." He leaned forward on the arms of the chair. "I will find them. I will punish them. If you don't help me, it will not go well for you."

"I really don't know where they are. We split up and I haven't heard from them."

He slapped her again. "You have betrayed the family."

Tears flowed from Huong's eyes. "Uncle –"

"Don't call me that. Not ever again. You are no longer part of this family. You are dead to me."

He turned and headed for the door. "You will stay in this house. You will not leave for any reason. I will instruct the guards to shoot on sight if you try to leave."

THE SLEEPING BAG was empty when Ted got up and pulled on his jeans and boots. He smelled the sultry aroma of coffee. He slipped off into the woods to relieve himself, then returned to camp.

"This is as far as we can take the bikes," he said as he approached Hope and Kathy at the fire.

"Good morning to you, too, *Hermano*," Hope said and held out a cup of coffee.

"Uh – yeah. Good morning." Ted sniffed the coffee. "This is what the gods drink in h

Heaven."

Like the others, Ted was a coffee snob. The dark Sumatra brew tickled his nostrils.

"What's the plan for today, chief?" Kathy asked.

Ted stretched. "We leave the bikes here. We can't take them any farther and besides, the noise would alert the whole jungle we're coming."

"Makes sense," Chris said as he emerged from his tent, shirtless.

Shit. Do you always need to show off your abs like that? "We'll put on our CAT suits to make sure no one sees us. We'll hike in from here," Ted said.

"Okay, Mr. Know-It-All," Hope teased. "How far do we have to hike?" She handed Ted a container with scrambled eggs and sausage.

"Mmm. Smells good."

"You haven't tasted it yet," Kathy said. "Freeze-dried food. No flavor at all."

"Answer my question," Hope chided.

"I don't know. We'll hike in until we find it."

"Don't make it sound so mysterious," Chris said. "We'll use

the GPS in our helmets to zero in on the camp. Angel will have a drone overhead to feed us live video of the camp."

"Thank God for your friend, Allison." Hope took a bite of her eggs and made a face. "Not like Mama used to make."

"They don't have any freeze-dried salsa, do they?" Ted asked.

"Okay," Kathy said. "So, we find the camp, then what?"

"We stake it out." Ted sipped his coffee. "We need to determine their habits and patterns. We need to figure out the best time to make our raid."

"Oh, God." Kathy tossed her hair over her shoulder. "You sound like a James Patterson novel."

They finished breakfast and broke camp.

"Let's slither into our CAT suits," Ted said.

Each camper retired to the jungle for privacy. They emerged in light blue body-tight suits with dark blue trim. The shoulders and upper chests were dark blue. A strip of gold piping separated the dark from the light areas.

"These things look like they were designed by Christian Dior," Kathy said.

"More like something from *Star Trek* if you ask me," Hope quipped.

Ted fiddled with his crotch to get comfortable. "I hope you remember the briefing Allison gave us." He pulled the experimental pistol from his holster.

He dropped out the magazine and checked that the cartridges were blue for tranquilizer darts. *Kathy's right. This isn't Mexico. If we kill someone, we'll be in a world of hurt.*

"Okay, now we're superheroes. What next?" Chris asked.

"Grab your backpacks," Ted said, "and let's go."

24

THE LONG HIKE IN — QUANG BINH PROVINCE, VIETNAM

The boots were extremely comfortable. The team made good progress through the jungle. The trail constricted and climbed over hills and crossed rivers.

Ted was amazed that as they waded across a stream, he felt totally dry. When he came out on the other side, the suit shed water instantly.

"Oh, God," Hope whispered and pointed. "A snake."

The foot and a half long snake looked different from any snake Ted had ever seen. It raised its head and flicked its tongue. When it lay still, the back was black and the belly a pink gray. When it moved, the scales flicked back and forth between green and blue, and it shone with iridescence.

"I don't think it's dangerous," Chris said. "With a broad head like that, it must be a constrictor."

The snake slithered away into the underbrush.

"It gives me the creeps," Hope said.

"C'mon, Indy," Ted teased. "I know you hate snakes."

"Don't worry, Hope," Kathy said. "If these suits can stop a bullet from an assault rifle, I'm sure they're impervious to snake bites"

"Whoa. Listen to this," Chris said. "I searched the Web through my helmet. It's a totally new species. Scientists only discovered it in 2019. They don't even have a common name for it yet. They call it *Achalinus zugorum*."

"Thank you, Mr. Wizard," Hope said and snuggled up to him with her arms around his waist.

They moved farther into the jungle. Bird calls filled the air, along with hoots, clicks, and the occasional roar. Ted was sure he heard the snarl of a big cat. *Is that you, Oscar?*

After a full day of hiking, Ted called a stop. "Let's set up camp before dark."

"We must have gone twenty miles today," Hope said.

Chris brought up the GPS application in his helmet. "Not quite. Eighteen point three miles to be exact."

"Thank you, Mr. Spock." Hope removed her helmet and shook out her long black hair.

"No fire tonight," Ted said. "We're getting close to the camp. They might see it."

"Crap," Chris said. "Cold food."

"Better cold food than hot lead," Hope replied.

Kathy became more and more withdrawn as the day went on. She sat on a log by herself.

Ted noticed and sat next to her. "Something wrong, Kath?"

She shook her head, but a tear appeared in her eye. "No, nothing."

Ted put his arm around her shoulder and pulled her close. "Something's not right in Denmark. You haven't been yourself all day."

Kathy melted into Ted's shoulder. "I guess – I guess I'm a little afraid." She sniffed.

"Of what?"

"I don't know. That's the problem. I don't know what's ahead of us. I'm afraid that you guys'll bust in there like cowboys and leave havoc in your wake." She shook her head and pulled away from Ted. Tears rolled down her cheeks. "I'm afraid that one or all of us will get killed or captured. Who knows what can happen?"

Ted pulled her back close again and wiped the tears from her face. "Kathy, we've done this before. We're very careful and we don't want to hurt anyone. Besides, Allison's CAT suits give us a huge advantage. They won't even know we're there."

Kathy sniffled and buried her face in Ted's chest.

THE TEAM ROSE AT DAYBREAK. They ate a cold breakfast and broke camp.

"We should go in stealth mode from here out. We don't want any guards spotting us." Ted turned on his CAT suit. "Computer, invisibility."

"Invisibility on, Ted," the computer responded.

He watched the other tree dissolve into the jungle. "Good. Computer, infrared."

"Infrared monitor on," the female voice responded.

He watched a red line run horizontally down his heads-up display. His three companions showed in red shapes on his screen. He was amazed at the amount of wildlife around him. With regular vision, they were invisible, but the infrared sensors picked them all up.

"Computer, open com." A little microphone icon appeared in the upper right-hand corner of his screen.

"Com open," the computer said.

I need to give her a name. It's like having a personal relationship with a person on the telephone.

Ted focused on the microphone icon and blinked twice, the equivalent of a double-click on a desktop computer. "Guardian Angel, this is Scout. Are you there?"

God, what would I do without Allison? Thank you for letting us use your support team.

"Roger that, Scout," a male voice replied.

Jesus, crap. It feels like he's talking inside my head.

"Angel, send up the drone. We're heading toward the camp. I want a visual of what's going on there."

"Roger that. Drone deployed."

"All right, kids. Let's rock and roll."

"Where is Angel and where is he sending the drone from?" Hope asked.

"He's in a secure location in Thailand."

"It's an experimental stealth drone being developed by Millennium Systems," Chris said. It cruises at nearly four hundred miles an hour, with a service ceiling at forty thousand feet and can stay in the air for fifteen hours."

"Mr. Wizard does it again," Hope chided.

"No, really, I saw some of the specs while were at their headquarters in Seattle."

"As long as it reaches the camp before we do," Ted said, "I'll be happy."

The four nearly invisible adventurers set out on the trail. When they stood still, they blended into the background so thoroughly a human eye couldn't detect them. When they moved, they created a wavy movement in the jungle background.

"This is so cool." Hope swiveled her head all around her as she walked. "We never saw any of these animals yesterday."

"Don't worry, sis. I'll keep an eye out for snakes."

"Rub it in."

The path was nothing more than a game trail.

"Computer, switch on GPS." *What should we name her?* "Hey, guys, we need to name the computer."

"Good idea," Kathy said. "It feels so personal talking to her."

"How about Nelly, as in 'Whoa, Nelly?'" Chris suggested.

"Nah, too old-fashioned sounding." Hope gave him a shove in the shoulder.

"Let's call her Phoc," Kathy said. "The Vietnamese god of blessings."

"Nope." Ted stepped over tree roots covering the trail. "She's not Vietnamese. She was built in the good old U. S. of A."

"So, what's your idea, smarty?" Kathy threaded through the tree roots.

"Hmm – I don't know. How about something like Marilyn or Madonna?"

"That's just lame, Bro." Chris followed the other three partners to watch their backs. "We need to go for something more – I don't know – modern."

Hope stopped to think a moment. "How about Emily? Or Lilly? Those are soft, nurturing names."

"I like Lilly," Kathy said.

"Me, too." Ted smiled inside his helmet. *Leave it to my little sister.* "Okay, Lilly it is. I'll program it into the system."

With that settled, the group continued to move quietly into the jungle.

Ted looked up at the microphone icon and blinked twice "Angel, you there?"

"Roger that."

"How's the bird doing?"

"It's making its way toward the GPS coordinates."

"Great, let us know when it's there."

"Roger, out."

Ted wanted to wipe his brow but realized he wasn't sweating. *It must be, what? Ninety degrees out there, a hundred?* Yet he was as comfortable as a Seattle summer day. *Damn, these CAT suits are amazing.*

They trudged on for another hour before their Guardian Angel called them again.

"I have visual on the target. I'm feeding it to your screens now."

The display on Ted's faceplate lit up with a jungle scene from above. Seemingly endless jungle surrounded a small clearing. Several buildings covered with camouflage netting and tree branches filled the clearing.

"Got it, Angel. Thanks."

Ted studied the image. It looked identical to the one Bear found in the DoD database.

"This might be it, gang." He turned to view his friends. "Looks like a viable target."

"Do you have to sound so military," Kathy chided. "I feel like I'm playing Army with a bunch of boys."

"I don't see any movement," Chris said. "The place looks practically deserted."

"Can we get an infrared image?" Hope asked. "I thought I saw something in the jungle at the periphery."

"Got ya. Lilly, switch to infrared."

"Infrared up, Ted."

Suddenly the screen came to life. Little red images moved throughout the jungle. Two big images moved together in harmony on the north side. Two more on the south side.

"Looks like guards," Chris said. "Two sets."

"I got 'em," Ted replied.

In the long, narrow building at the south edge there were six more figures. In the central building was a single heat image.

"*Jesus Christo*. Is that him?" Ted asked.

"There's only one way to find out, Amigo." Chris pointed down the trail. "Let's get there and see."

They walked in silence for the next hour, each friend lost in their own thoughts.

"Stop." Ted held a fist in the air. "I think we're closing in on the guards.

Chris knelt down on one knee. "If we're quiet, it shouldn't be any problem slipping past them with these outfits."

Ted stopped to study the aerial image once again. "We still got the two on the north and two on the south. The ones in the building aren't moving much."

"Let's split the difference," Hope said. "And go in from the west."

"Works for me. Okay, troops, let's move." Ted led the four

south for a couple of hundred yards, then turned east. "That should be far enough. Now, everybody, you gotta be totally silent."

They took slow steps toward the camp. Each friend putting their weight on one foot quietly before stepping forward with the next.

"There it is, Teddy." Kathy pointed forward.

Shit. That's the first time she's called me "Teddy."

"Let's park it here and watch for a while." Ted squatted down.

They observed the camp silently for almost an hour. There was no sign of movement. Their drone moved slowly around the camp perimeter, feeding them information.

"It looks like nothing's happening. Let's move out." Ted stood and silently moved toward the camp.

"God, this feels weird." Chris still trailed the two women. "I feel totally exposed, walking right into their camp. But I know they can't see me."

"We'll head for the prison building." Sweat trickled down Ted's forehead, but not from the heat.

25

BAO'S REVENGE — HANOI

Colonel Bao paced his office, back and forth between his huge teak desk and the equally impressive credenza. Trappings of his power filled the room. Photographs covered the walls. Pictures of Bao grinning and gladhanding various political and military figures. A photo of a group of Vietnamese people crowded around a dead American flyer. A picture of Bao shooting a Vietnamese man in the head. The timing was impeccable. The photographer captured the moment the bullet entered the skull and blasted out the back of the head.

Vietnamese flags flanked either side of his desk. Framed letters and certificates covered one wall.

He mumbled as he paced. "That little slut," he hissed. "She betrayed me. After all I've done for her."

The door opened and a uniformed woman led Huong into the office.

"Leave us," Bao commanded.

Huong looked like she had little sleep. Her dress was ruffled and her hair messy. Black streaks ran down her cheeks where her mascara ran while she cried.

"So – have you had time to consider your position?"

"Uncle, ah – sir, I don't have anything to tell you. They aren't spies so I can't report anything incriminating to you."

Bao slapped her across the face.

Huong stumbled but kept her footing.

"You liar. You traitor. You have shamed this family –"

"Please, Uncle. I've done nothing wrong."

He faced the window with his hands clasped behind his back. "You are a traitor. You have stabbed a dagger into my heart. You have nothing more to say?"

She dropped to her knees, tears streaming down her dirty face. "I don't know anything to tell you. What do you want? I'll tell you anything."

Bao spun and faced her. "Who are they, really? What are they doing in Vietnam? Where have they gone?"

Tears flowed freely. "Uncle, I don't know – "

"Stop calling me that. I am not your uncle. I am the Head of State Security."

"—I only know what Kathy told me. They are Americans on vacation in Vietnam. Kathy wanted to show Ted her country."

"Enough lies." Bao kicked her in the head.

Huong sprawled on the floor and moaned. "That's what they told me. If there's some other reason for being here, I don't know it."

He bent down and grabbed Huong's collar. He raised her to her feet and held her face inches from his. "Where have they gone?"

His breath reeked of fish and garlic. "I don't know. They didn't tell me. I only know that Ted said something about finding his uncle."

"His uncle? Hmmm – what could that mean?"

"I don't know."

"Enough, I'm done with you." He reached to push the button on the intercom on his desk. "Send in the guard."

Almost instantly, the door opened, and the uniformed woman walked into the room.

"Take her away." Bao turned his back on Huong again. He stood motionless staring out the window.

"Uncle – "

The woman grabbed Huong's bicep and marched her out of the room.

BREAKING IN — QUANG BINH PROVINCE

The first obstacle was a high, barbed-wire fence.

"Lilly," Ted asked, "is the fence electrified?"

"I cannot detect any current in the fence," said the automaton voice.

"Is it connected to any alarm system?"

"No, Ted. However, I detect sensors in the killing field between the fence and the stone wall."

"Shit." Ted bent over with his hands on his knees to catch his breath. "You guys get that?"

"Yeah, Bro." Chris moved alongside Ted. "Can't we get the HUD to show us the sensors?"

"I'll try. Lilly, show us the sensors on our displays."

A red horizontal line moved down their screens. Little orange blobs appeared every six feet along the perimeter.

"We shouldn't have any trouble moving past those," Hope said.

Ted raised his hand, palm out. "What if they're motion detectors? Will our suits still work?"

"I don't know," Chris answered. "We had a case last year where our client sued the security company because their system didn't warn them of a home invasion." He pulled up the brief up in the screen that floated in his eidetic memory. "Let's see. They were infrared sensors. They're set off when a heat signature moves through their area."

"But are these infrared?" Kathy asked. "Are there other kinds?"

"I don't know," Chris replied. "Infrared and ultrasonic are the two main types, but there are a handful of others." He looked at Ted's heat signature. "Ted, can you find out?"

"Lilly, are these sensors infrared?"

It took a second for Lilly to respond. "Yes, Ted. They're Capricorn 2000s. Infrared sensors."

"Great. Will our suits protect us from the sensors?"

"Yes, Ted. Your CAT suits not only control the heat inside your suit, they control the energy given off by your heat signature. I can turn it down so that you will be virtually invisible to infrared sensors."

Ted pumped his arm. "Ka-chiiing. Lilly, do it. Turn down our heat signatures."

"Very well but you should know that it will put an extra drain on your batteries. Instead of twelve hours, you will only get four hours out of a charge."

"Do it."

Ted reached in his backpack and pulled out a set of wire cutters. He snipped a hole in the barbed wire and held it open for the others.

When they were all through, they froze and waited to see if they would be detected.

No alarms, no guards rushing around. They were in.

Each moved slowly and carefully as they approached the wall. Hope took a folding grapple from her pack, opened it, attached a rope to it, and flung it over the wall. It held.

Chris went first. He pulled himself up the rope like a mountain climber ascending a cliff. After Chris, Hope went. She struggled more than Chris.

"Here, Honey, let me pull you up." Chris took the rope and hauled up her one hundred-fifty pounds.

Kathy scampered up the rope like a monkey. Ted went last to keep an eye out for guards.

When the four were on top of the wall, they reversed the grapple and repelled down inside the compound. Once again, they huddled soundlessly by the wall and waited. No sign of anyone detecting them.

"Where to now, Boss?" Kathy asked.

"Ted pointed toward a concrete building in the center of the compound. "That central building must be the prison." He didn't realize that the others couldn't make out where he was pointing.

"Okay, let's head out." Chris took a deep breath. "Be in ultra-stealth mode. It wouldn't be good if we got caught now."

The four moved silently and invisibly to the building. There was a lock on the door.

"*Hermano*, this looks like your specialty," Hope said.

Ted moved up and examined the lock. He took the pick set out of his thigh pocket and went to work. In thirty seconds the lock clicked, and he opened the door.

They looked into a small lobby with a guard station on their right. A lazy guard looked up as the door opened.

"Hello?" he said in Vietnamese.

The four froze.

The guard got up and walked out from his station. Ted and Hope flattened themselves against the right wall, Chris and Kathy on the left.

The guard reached the door, stepped through, and looked around. He saw nothing.

Ted held his breath. *Surely the guard can hear my heart pounding.*

The four snuck past the guard and into the lobby.

The guard turned, closed the door, and headed back to his station. He picked up a girlie magazine and went back to his fantasies.

Ted led his friends down the corridor. As they tiptoed past each door, they looked in and found them empty.

The sixth cell had a man in it. He was large, with long red hair and beard. He sat on his bunk reading.

"That can't be Gino." Ted felt disappointment in his chest.

"Let's see if there's anyone else," Chris said.

The four split up and searched the other cells. All were empty.

"He's the only one," Kathy said.

"Who is he? Why's he here alone?" Hope asked.

"Only one way to find out."

Ted picked the lock on the door and opened it.

The big man shot to his feet and looked at the empty door. He took a couple of steps to the door and looked around.

"Don't worry," Ted said. "We're here to help you."

The red-headed giant patted his ears with the palm of his hands.

"Oh, sorry." Ted lifted the faceplate on his helmet.

"What the hell?" The tall man said in English as a pair of dark brown eyes materialized in front of him.

HUONG BOUNCED along in the back of an Army truck with eleven other dissidents. Where they were going and what was going to happen to them was anyone's guess.

The two armed guards in the back of the truck wouldn't talk to them. They acted as if the prisoners were diseased.

Huong sat on the long bench seat and sobbed.

"Why are you here?" the girl next to her asked.

"I don't know. My uncle thinks I betrayed my country." There was a long silence. Finally, Huong spoke. "I didn't. I love my country. I would do anything for my country. He asked me about things I know nothing about. Then he sent me to jail."

The bumpy ride came to an end. Huong and the other prisoners were hustled out of the truck.

They were at an airfield. Military jets lined the taxiways and helicopters huddled in front of huge hangars.

"Move," one of the guards said as he shoved the butt of his rifle into a prisoner's ribs.

The guards herded the group to a helicopter and forced them to climb aboard.

The guards on the helicopter handcuffed each prisoner's hands behind their backs.

"Where are we going? Huong asked.

No one replied.

The side door slid shut and the engines began to spin. The noise in the cargo area of the helicopter deafened Huong.

There were no seats, so Huong and the other prisoners lowered themselves to the floor.

Huong felt the big bird lift into the air.

What's happening to us? Where are they taking us?

The chopper tilted to the right, then sped up. No one tried to talk over the noise.

The ride lasted about an hour, then the helicopter hovered. One of the guards opened the sliding cargo door. Wind from the rotors blasted into the cargo bay. The other guard motioned for the prisoners to get to their feet.

Huong saw water below them. *We must be over the ocean. Are we going to an island? Maybe a ship? But why?*

The guard shoved a woman in the back with his rifle. The woman fell out of the door, screaming. Before anyone had a chance to react, the other guard shoved another prisoner out the door.

Panic broke out. The prisoners fought to stay in the aircraft. The guards struck them with their rifles. The prisoners wouldn't budge. One guard shot a dissident and shoved him out the door.

The guards smashed at their charges. People fell to the deck and the guards shoved them out the door.

Huong screamed. A guard shoved her with his rifle barrel. She tried to resist, but he was too strong. She stumbled forward and fell out the door.

She screamed as she fell. She was on her back looking up at the helicopter and the blue sky.

"Nooooooo."

She hit the water after dropping two thousand feet. Her head snapped back and hit the surface of the water, which was as hard as concrete.

Then everything went black.

BREAKING OUT – QUANG BINH PROVINCE

"We're wearing invisibility suits," Ted said to the big man, then turned to his companions. "Keep your invisibility on. Lilly, turn off my invisibility."

The prisoner gasped as Ted materialized out of the air.

"What are you?"

"I'm Ted Higuera. I'm a PI from Seattle. I have three friends here with me, but they're staying cloaked in case someone comes by."

The big man, unkept, his pale, freckled face sallow and gaunt, stared with confusion.

"We're going to get you out of here. I heard rumors of a prisoner still being held in Vietnam. I hoped it might be my uncle. But we'll get you out anyway."

"Out?" the red headed man said in a squeaky voice.

"Yeah, we're going to take you home." Ted looked over his shoulder. He knew he had three friends watching his back, but he kept looking around anyway. "What's your name?"

The big man slumped back onto his bed. "Gunnar Torvelsen."

"How long have you been here?"

"I don't know. I was captured in 69."

"Shit, that's over fifty years ago."

Gunnar wiped his eyes. "It was a lifetime ago."

Ted sat on the bed next to Gunnar. "How did you get here? Why have they held you so long?"

Gunnar shook his head. "I was a Green Beret. We were on a top-secret mission in North Vietnam. Someone leaked our mission, and they were waiting for us. Only Gino and I made it out."

Ted grabbed Gunnar's shirt by the shoulders. "GINO? Gino Higuera?"

"Yeah, the Taco Man."

"You know Gino?"

"Yeah, he was our master sergeant."

"Holy Christ. We came halfway round the world to find him. What happened to him?"

Gunnar took a deep breath and stared back through the decades. "Gino was hit. Bad. We were in the same hospital. I don't know how he survived."

"But he's alive?" Ted crept forward to the edge of the bed.

"I – don't – know. They took him away."

"Where? Why?"

Gunnar shook his head.

"Why are you still here? Vietnam returned all the POWs ages ago."

Gunnar stood, walked to the wall, and looked up at the heavy bars on the window. "I remember when they let everyone else go home. Them sons-a-bitches wouldn't let me go."

"But why?"

"I guess they didn't want anyone to hear my story."

Ted looked back at his invisible friends. "Your story? What did you do?"

"It wasn't me, it was us. My whole A-team." He turned to face Ted. "We were snuck into North Vietnam to Hanoi. We met up with sympathizers along the way. They helped us. Someone musta ratted us out." Tears formed at the corners of his eyes.

"Me and Gino were the hitters. Our mission was to assassinate Ho Chi Minh."

"Holy God." Ted tried to wipe his forehead but hit his helmet.

"We got the bastard. But we lost the whole A-team."

"No, that's impossible," Chris said.

Gunnar's head swiveled toward the disembodied voice.

"Ho Chi Minh died of a heart attack. I remember reading about it."

"That can't be. I saw his head fly apart." Gunner searched for the source of Chris's voice. "I guess that could be a cover story they made up so that G2 wouldn't know we succeeded."

"Crap." Ted put a hand on Gunnar's shoulder. "You really assassinated Ho Chi Minh?"

"Yeah. Fat lot of good it did us."

"But what happened to my Uncle Gino?"

THE JUNGLE WAS hot and fetid. The Americans surrounded them. How did they find them? They always outsmarted the occidental fools.

Bao clung to his AK-47 and watched for movement in the jungle. The GIs hadn't spotted them yet.

Those fools. They could walk right past me and not see a thing.

With branches tied to his back, Bao melted into the jungle.

Then a gunshot. Then another. The Americans opened up with automatic weapons. Bao could tell the difference between the sound of the Yankees' M-16s and the Chinese AK-47s.

The AK-47s roared back. A full-scale firefight. Enemy fire pinned down his platoon.

The newly-minted lieutenant didn't know what to do.

"Hold your fire," he whispered to his sergeant who passed the order along. "I don't think they've seen us yet."

They were outnumbered at least five to one. Maybe more.

Two Vietnamese soldiers popped up not twenty meters from Bao and hosed down the Yankees. The Americans were brave. Those that still stood returned fire and the Vietnamese men went down. The firefight continued. Both sides taking heavy casualties.

Bao's comm man handed him the radio receiver and said, "Colonel Dinh."

"Yes, Colonel."

"Bao, where are you. Are you taking any casualties?"

Bao took a deep breath. "We're right in the middle of their detachment. We're camouflaged and they haven't seen us yet."

"You're what? We're right in the middle of a battle and you're cowering in the underbrush?"

A pregnant silence hung between them.

"You will attack at once, Lieutenant. That's an ORDER."

Boa dropped the receiver. *It's suicide.* His commander ordered his men and him to commit suicide. For what?

He sighted his rifle on an American's back. "Open fire!" He pulled the trigger.

The jungle around him erupted in gunfire. Many of the enemy went down, but so did his men. A grenade exploded near him, three of his soldiers flew through the air. Various body parts followed them. The concussion hit him like a charging *va quang* ox, the air forced from his lungs. He blacked out momentarily.

When he opened his eyes, everything looked foggy. Stars filled his vision.

The air in front of him seemed to shimmer. He tried to clear his eyes. Two dark-brown eyes appeared in front of him.

"Bao, you killed your own niece. Now you're going to pay."

Bao screamed and sat up in bed. Sweat poured down his face, his heart wild. He clenched and unclenched his fists.

What is it? Bao never felt remorse. Yet, he had Huong killed, but it was for the good of the state. Everything he did was for the good of the state.

So why this dream? Why that battle?

He had been wounded and sent back to North Vietnam. After

his recovery, he led a new platoon to the South. He had been spectacular at killing Americans.

Why dream of it now? And the eyes. Whose eyes were they? They just hung there in space, not attached to a body.

He knew that voice. Where had he heard it before?

GETTIN' *out ain't gonna be as easy as gettin' in,* Ted thought as he turned on his invisibility and led his band out of the cell.

There was still only one guard at the entrance to the building. "We're gonna have to take him out," Ted said.

"No," Kathy objected. "We can't hurt him. There has to be another way."

"Take it easy, Dragon Lady. We're just going to use tranquilizer darts."

"Are you sure that won't hurt him?"

Ted ignored Kathy's question. "Hope, you're our best shot. You need to creep up and put the guy down."

"Roger that, *Mi Capitán.*" Hope gave a mock salute and tiptoed forward.

Ted watched from the hallway. Gunnar was safely around the corner, out of sight.

Hope got to within ten feet of the guard and unholstered her weapon. She aimed. The gun made a faint thawp sound.

The guard grabbed at the dart and slumped to the ground.

"Get the dart," he yelled to Hope. "C'mon you guys, let's vamoose."

At the entrance to the building, Ted stopped to survey the compound. There was no one on the grounds.

"I still have six Tangos in the barracks," Chris said.

Ted took a deep breath. "Okay, let's go."

He went first, followed by Hope, pistol still in hand. Then

came Kathy and Gunnar, running with a pronounced limp. Finally, Chris came last, covering their backs.

At the wall, Ted found the rope hanging down. He shimmied up the wall, followed by Kathy. Hope grabbed the rope and started up the wall. As before, she made slow progress.

"Hold on, Sis. I'll pull you up."

He took the rope and started to pull it up, hand over hand. "Geeze, Sis. Have you been swallowing rocks?"

"Very funny, *pendejo*. You're putting on a belly yourself."

He hauled her to the top of the wall and dropped the rope down. The three balanced on the foot-thick wall.

"Okay, Gunnar, you're next."

Gunnar took the rope and looked up at the wall. "I don't think I can make it. My knee is shot up, and I don't get any exercise."

"We'll help you," Ted whispered down. "Hope, the piton and pulley."

Hope unzipped her bag and pulled out a steel spike with a loop at the top. She handed that and a hammer to her brother.

Ted took the tool and started pounding the spike into the top of the concrete wall.

"Ted," Hope exclaimed. "They must be able to hear that ringing for a mile."

Ted looked at the hammer in his hand. "I don't have any other ideas to get Gunnar up. Do you?" He looked at Hope and Kathy.

"Well, no," Hope said.

Ted continued to drive the piton into the wall. When it was secure, he held out his hand and Hope passed him a block and tackle.

After attaching the block to the piton, Ted dropped one end of the rope to Chris and dangled the other end on the front side of the wall. "How much do you weigh, compadre?" he asked Gunnar.

"I don't know. I used to weigh two forty, but that was a long time ago."

Chris took the dropped line and tied a loop in the bottom.

"Here, put this under your arms." He looped the rope over Gunnar's head. "Grab the rope and try to walk your way up the wall. Ted and the girls will hoist you up."

"You guys grab onto the rope and go over the wall," Ted said to Hope and Kathy. "That'll give us a head start."

Gunnar lifted off the ground. He managed to get his feet on the wall and as Ted pulled on the rope, he inched up the wall.

Ted heard the shout before he saw the guard.

A spotlight swept the compound and came to rest on Gunnar, climbing up the wall.

Guards poured out of the barracks with rifles in hand.

"Oh, shit. Girls, help me pull the rope."

Gunshots rang out. Ted and the girls pulled frantically. Gunnar moved up the wall; bullets sending pieces of concrete and dust everywhere.

Chris dropped to his knee, pulled his gun, and held it with two hands. He'd been raised around guns and quickly dropped one of the guards.

The experimental pistol showed virtually no barrel flash. Chris was invisible in the spotlight's illumination. The guards looked around frantically for the source of the fire.

The guards shouted and switched to automatic fire. Bullets flew around Gunnar's head.

Ted reached down and grabbed the former Green Beret's hand, pulled him over the top and shoved him down the other side. "Get down fast. They can see you."

Gunnar rappelled down the wall.

Chris took the rope and began climbing up the wall.

The guards couldn't see him, but they noticed the rope moving around. They fired. Chris yelled and fell.

Ted dropped to the ground beside Chris. "You okay, compadre?"

Chris groaned and rubbed his back. "Yeah. Thank God for these suits. That hurt."

Ted helped his friend up and over the wall, then followed him down.

"We need to get out of here pronto," Ted said as his feet hit the ground.

"You betcha," Gunnar said.

"Stop," Hope yelled. "They have security cameras everywhere."

"We can't sneak past them with Gunnar," Ted said as he surveyed the killing zone. "We just have to go."

Kathy and Ted helped Gunnar limp across the field to their hole in the fence.

Guards came around the corner and opened fire.

Hope and Chris returned fire, dropping two guards.

Gunnar was through the fence, Kathy and Ted helped him to the jungle.

Chris and Hope scampered across the field and through the fence.

Bullets continued to whiz around them.

"Into the forest." Chris yelled. "Fast."

They moved as fast as they could in the dark with a limping old man.

The sound of a truck's engine caused Kathy to turn around. "Oh, God. There's a bunch more of them."

As they moved deeper into the jungle, Ted heard the sounds of Vietnamese infantry pursuing.

"Lilly," Ted shouted to his helmet. "Find us a place to hide."

"There is a large cave five kilometers to your northwest," Lilly said in a calm voice.

"Five K," Ted said to Gunnar. "Can you make it?"

"Damned straight. I make it or die trying."

They continued to the northwest as the sun peeked over the eastern horizon, occasionally hearing gunshots. They soon lost sight of their trackers.

Time passed and the meters fell away. Ted led and hacked

away at the jungle with his machete. As air conditioned as his CAT suit was, he was drenched in sweat.

He estimated they had covered five kilometers when Lilly said, "You have arrived at your destination. The cave is on your left."

Ted turned to his left. There was no cave. He took a few steps to a wall of solid foliage. He pulled at it and tugged it away from a rock wall. He continued to move down the wall as his friends joined in the hunt.

"It's here," Kathy shouted and pulled the vegetation from the wall.

Ted ran over and saw the opening. "Jesus, you could park a Mac truck in here."

Gunnar's breath came in loud gasps. He bent over and put his hands on his knees. "This is too much for an old fart like me. How we gonna get outta here?"

Ted put an arm around his shoulder and led him to a rock where he collapsed. "We're going to hide out here until nightfall. Then we'll make our way back to the road. We'll rendezvous with one of Giang's friends there."

GUNNAR'S STORY – QUANG BINH PROVINCE

T ed sat on a rock near Gunnar and watched him eat. Gunnar tore into one of the freeze-dried meals. The man had lived on fish and rice for decades. Even the packaged meal was a banquet to him.

"So, you knew my Uncle Gino?" Ted asked.

Gunnar took a drink of water and wiped his mouth on his wrist. "Yeah. He was our top sergeant. Me and him were on the sniper team. He was my spotter."

Ted just sat and looked at the bent old man. He could hardly picture him as a robust, young Green Beret. "What happened to him?"

"We were both shot up pretty bad. They took us to a field hospital. The soldiers weren't too anxious for us to get treatment, but the doctors and nurses refused to let us die." Gunnar's eyes went blank, as if he were looking into the dim past.

"We were friends. We were all friends. Anyone on the A-team would gladly lay down his life for another." Gunnar's eyes dampened. "His best friend was a guy called Mo. Short for Mohammed I think." Gunnar stopped and looked off into space.

After a moment, Ted prodded him. "Go on."

"Ah – we trained for this mission in Laos. They had a camp there. There was an exact replica of the Imperial Citadel and buildings around it. We trained for weeks. We tried all of the buildings looking for the best place to take the shot."

The team was all enrapt by this point.

"We were smuggled into the North by South Vietnamese sympathizers. There were lots of them. The people in the countryside hated the communists." Gunnar took a deep breath. "Anyway, we made it to Hanoi. We deployed exactly as planned. Everything went according to plan until zero hour."

Gunnar furrowed his brows, a sneer found its way to his lips, his eyes seemed to glow in the semi-darkness.

"Them bastards. Someone leaked our mission. The Gooks knew we were coming."

Kathy looked as if she had been slapped in the face.

"They were ready for us." He spat on the ground. "They had soldiers waiting at every spot we picked out. They cut us down like dogs."

"But you said you shot Ho Chi Minh?" Hope asked.

"Yeah, me and Gino were on top of the building. I was sighting in on the old bastard when the soldiers broke in. Gino tried to hold them off, but there were just too many of them. There was no cover on the roof."

He paused again. Ted could see him reliving the past.

After a long moment Gunnar spoke again. "I got off the shot. I saw the back of Uncle Ho's head blow apart. Then they got me. I don't know how many times I was hit, but I blacked out. When I woke up, I was in a hospital. Like I said, the doctors and nurses refused to let us die."

Gunnar got up and walked to the cave entrance. He leaned against the rocks and looked out.

"Gino was in a bad way. They assigned this Vietnamese girl to take care of us. She changed our bandages, brought us food and water, and cleaned up after our waste. She was a nice girl."

Gunnar turned back to the group. "She and Gino fell in love. I think it was his love for her that got him through. I wouldn't a given a snowball's chance that he'd survive, but he pulled through."

"Geeze," Ted said.

"What happened to her?" Hope asked.

"She served us for years. I don't know how long. I don't know what day it is, what year. It was just a long time."

Hope was leaning forward from her seat in the dirt. "Then what?"

"They took him away. They never told me why or where they took him. They just came for him one day and I was all alone. A long time passed, and they took all the other prisoners away, leaving just me in the camp. Then a lot more years passed."

Ted grabbed Gunnar by the biceps and pulled him close. "Then what happened? Where's my uncle?"

"I don't know, Ted." Gunnar pulled free. "From time to time I'd pick up a rumor or a bit of the guard's conversation, but I don't know how much of it was true."

"TELL ME!" Ted grabbed Gunnar's collar. "What did you hear?"

Gunnar took a deep breath and answered in a soft voice. "I heard that Gino was paroled to the girl's custody. They said he went with her to her father's farm somewhere out in the pucker brush. That's all I know. That was a lot of years ago. Even if it's true, I don't know what the chances are that he's still alive."

SIX MEN in Army fatigues hunched down around a pile of money on the garage floor. The big open space reeked of oil, gasoline, and cigarette smoke. A beat-up old panel truck sat inside the door.

The men just stared at the money.

"Have you ever seen anything like this?" an older man asked.

"That's more money that I thought existed in the whole world," a man with a long scar running down the left side of his face said.

A good-looking young man rose to his feet. "We did it. We never have to work again."

"You mean you don't want to hijack another load?" Scarface asked.

"We're pushing our luck as it is. We need to take our money and get out of Vietnam. Colonel Bao will never stop looking for us."

"But it was so easy –"

An explosion rocked the roll up door. Soldiers burst through the ragged opening. Gunfire erupted.

"On the floor," the officer shouted. "On your faces."

The six men complied immediately.

The soldiers crowded around the captives. The ringing in their ears cleared. A dread silence fell over the garage.

Colonel Bao walked through the still smoking opening. "Well, well. What have we here?"

He walked up to the old man and kicked him in the head.

"Aghhhh –"

"So you think you can out smart me? You think you can take what is mine?"

The prisoners made no sound.

Bao pointed to one man. "This one. Stand him up."

Two soldiers grabbed the man under the armpits and hoisted him to his feet.

"There," Bao said. "Against the wall."

The soldiers dragged the man to the wall.

Bao paused and looked at the man. The man's knees shook.

"Who's the leader here?" Bao asked.

The man didn't respond.

Bao quietly moved in front of the man. "I asked you a question." He slugged the man in the gut.

The man cried out and doubled over. The soldiers held him up.

"Let's get this straight. When I ask you a question, you answer me."

"Go to hell," the man said.

Without a word, Bao pulled his pistol and shot the man in the head.

"Next," he said to his soldiers.

The soldiers picked up the older man and stood him against the wall.

"I hope you will be more cooperative," Bao said as he rubbed the barrel of his gun against the man's cheek.

The old man lost control of his bladder. Dampness spread down the front of his pants and a puddle formed at his feet.

Bao slapped the man across the face with his pistol. "You decrepit old man. Now you will answer my questions."

The old man shook and sputtered. "It was the Mexican woman. She hired us."

"The Mexican woman?" Bao stepped back and thought. "The drug queen from Mexico?"

"Yes, that's it." The old man shit his britches. "They called her the queen."

"Damn it. Her again. She won't last to see the new moon." He put his gun up alongside the old man's head and fired.

One by one, Bao dispatched his prisoners without learning anything more.

"Shit." Bao holstered his pistol. "They were just lackies. We need to find a way to stop this Mexican woman. She must be connected to the Americans."

He turned and walked out of the garage. His men scooped up the money and put it in a duffle bag.

Thu, Bao's tall, thin aide, stood by the baby-blue Chevy Impala convertible. "I have a dispatch for you." He handed Bao a piece of paper.

Bao read the document. "Damn, when did this happen?" he asked Thu.

"This morning, sir. I just got the word."

"The Americans. It must be the Americans. We must find them. They can never leave the country with this news."

TED RAISED his fist and whispered, "Stop," into his helmet.

His three partners immediately halted, but Gunnar kept walking. Kathy grabbed Gunnar's arm and whispered to him. "Freeze. Ted sees something up ahead."

Gunnar did as told.

Ted crept forward. *This has to be it.* He peered out of the jungle to a small clearing. A stream tumbled over a cliff and fell forty or fifty feet into a clear, blue pool. *We meet Giang here.*

"Let's be real quiet, but I think this is our rendezvous," he said.

They emerged from the foliage and reveled in the mid-day sun.

"That water looks incredible," Kathy said.

"This is like a postcard from paradise," Hope added.

"I'm going in." Kathy removed her helmet and her head appeared. Her long black hair was matted to her head. "I could use a wash."

Ted watched as first one, then another foot appeared as Kathy took off her boots. Then her shoulders appeared as she shimmied out of her suit.

God damn, that's sexy.

Kathy wriggled out of her CAT suit and stood in her underwear. The suit became visible as Kathy removed it.

"Me, too." Hope's head appeared as she took off her helmet.

Then Chris appeared.

What the hell. Ted slithered out of his suit.

Kathy removed her bra and panties and jumped into the pool. "Woohoo."

Hope was right behind her. "Aieeee."

Ted stood shocked. He hadn't seen his sister naked since she was a baby.

Chris followed the women.

Ted shrugged, stripped down and dove after his friends.

Gunnar stood watching. Then started removing his clothes.

The cool water caressed Ted's skin. It felt incredibly good.

They played and splashed around in the water for a while, then Hope climbed out and found a flat rock to lie on and dry off.

"A very stirring performance," a voice said from the undergrowth.

Ted sprang to his suit and drew his pistol.

"Put that away. It's just me." Giang emerged from the woods. "I have made arrangements to get you out of the country."

"We're not done yet." Ted pulled on his boxers. "We freed Gunnar, but my uncle wasn't there. Gunnar thinks he lives back in the bush somewhere."

Giang sat on a downed log. "Hmm – well, we can get him out of the country." He pointed at Gunnar.

"Where will he go?" Kathy asked.

"We can get him into Cambodia. From there he'll go to the American Embassy."

"So, what do we do about Uncle Gino?" Ted asked.

"What do you know about him?" Giang asked.

"Not very much," Ted repeated Gunnar's story.

"I can ask around."

THE SEARCH CONTINUES –
QUANG BINH PROVINCE

Giang led the team to a remote farming village. There he introduced them to an old Vietnamese woman.

"*Chao chi,*" Kathy said to the woman as she took the woman's wrinkled hand in her own and bowed slightly.

They had a long exchange in Vietnamese. Ted shifted his weight from foot to foot nervously.

"She's heard of an ancient American living in a village not far from here," Kathy said, turning to Ted.

"Is it – ?"

"She doesn't know. She says he has lived there since the war."

Giang cut in and spoke to the woman in Vietnamese.

The woman took a step back and replied.

"She says the village is about half a day's hike from here," Giang said.

"We need to get going." Ted turned and reached for his backpack.

Chris grabbed his arm. "Hold on, partner. We don't know anything about this village yet. We could be walking into a trap. How about we spend the afternoon researching this and leave first thing in the morning?"

Chris is right. Ted nodded, rustled around in his backpack, and pulled out his cybernetic helmet. He jammed it on his head and connected it to their VPN.

Chris did the same while Kathy and Hope toured the village and met the people.

Ted looked at the microphone icon on his HUD. He blinked twice. "Angel, are you with me?"

"I'm here, Ted. What's up?"

"We have a change of plans. We're diverting to a small village to see if my uncle is there." He gave Angel the latitude and longitude. "Could you do a flyover and check the place out for us?"

"Sure, but it's getting a little late in the day. Why don't we do this first thing in the morning?"

TED and his crew were up with first light. So was the rest of the village.

They had tea and a quick bowl of rice with the old woman's family and were on their way. Giang remained behind in the village.

"We better change batteries," Ted said. "We don't want to run out of juice in the middle of an action."

They hiked through rice paddies and forested land. About an hour into their trek, Ted double blinked on his microphone icon.

"Angel, you with me?"

"Roger that, Ted. I have the Guardian Angel in the sky. It should be in place in about an hour."

Sounds about right. It's coming from Thailand.

The hike continued.

"Ted, Angel."

"Come in, Angel." Ted checked the clock in his HUD. It was almost exactly an hour since he last spoke to Angel.

"I'm in range now. I'll push the video to your HUD."

"Roger that," Ted said.

Almost instantly, the image of a tiny village appeared on Ted's screen. It was an aerial shot from about five thousand feet.

He could see the ubiquitous hooches. Corrals for the animals. People moving around. The village was surrounded by rice paddies. The farmers were already at work.

"Looks clear to me, Angel."

"Roger that. I don't see any signs of danger," Angel confirmed. "Angel out."

They entered the village about noon. Villagers ran to see who these strangers were. As foreigners in the backcountry, they might as well have been Klingons.

A hard-looking, middle-aged man approached them.

"*Chao anh*," Kathy said and bowed slightly. She did not extend her hand.

"*Chao em,*" the man replied.

"We are looking for an American," Kathy said in Vietnamese.

"There are many Americans in Vietnam," the man said.

"This one has been here since the American War." Kathy looked up at the man. "He was a prisoner, then was released to a Vietnamese man's custody."

Ted couldn't understand the conversation but could see the gears in the man's head working.

"I know of no such man."

Kathy nodded and swallowed. "We were told he was here. We were told that he had a family and a farm here."

The man stared at Kathy for a moment. "Who told you these lies?"

"An old woman in a village not far from here."

"Who are you?" the man asked.

"My name is Nguyen Hein." Kathy pointed to the team. "These are my friends. This is Ted, he's searching for his uncle."

Ted heard his name and perked up. "What's he saying?"

"He says he never heard of an American living here." Kathy turned to Ted and lowered her voice. "He's lying."

She turned back to the Vietnamese man. "Maybe you know him better as a Mexican. He is this man's uncle." Kathy pushed Ted forward.

The man seemed to waver. He held up a hand and walked to a group of elderly Vietnamese men. They conversed.

"How can you prove that this is true?"

Kathy glanced at Ted. "He wants proof that Gino's your uncle."

Ted reached into his pocket, pulled out a small velvet pouch, and handed it to Kathy.

Kathy poured out the contents and presented them to the man. "Here are his dog tags. I don't know what else we could do to convince you."

The man took the dog tags, studied them, then returned to the group of elders. They talked among themselves in hushed tones.

The man walked back and addressed Ted.

"He says they will trust you." Kathy put a hand on Ted's arm. "He says he doesn't agree, but the council has spoken."

The man spoke to Kathy again. "I know the man you seek. He is working in his fields now. He will be back this evening."

Kathy translated.

"No." Ted stepped forward. "We can't wait."

Kathy asked the man where they could find the American.

"He says that Gino's paddies are about two kilometers south of here," Kathy translated. "Do you want to go?"

"Yes. I came halfway around the world for this."

THE MILE WENT QUICKLY. Ted stood on the crest of a small hill looking down toward terraced rice paddies.

"God, I'm getting tired of walking," Hope said. "When we get home my feet are never going to touch the ground again."

"Oh, quit complaining, Sis. We're almost there." Ted looked down into the fields. An old man in a conical straw hat bent over the paddy doing something under water.

Is that him?

Ted couldn't even tell if the man was Vietnamese or Mexican. He was about Ted's height, which was slightly taller than the average Vietnamese. He was thin and wiry. Ted couldn't picture anyone from his family being thin.

"Hello," Ted shouted as he started down the hill.

The man stood straight and shaded his eyes with his right hand.

"Gino Higuera?" Ted asked.

The man answered something in Vietnamese.

"He says 'who are you?'" Kathy translated.

"Ted. Uncle Gino, I'm you're nephew, Ted."

The old man turned his gaze to Kathy. She translated.

As Ted got closer, he got a better look at the man. Definitely not Vietnamese. He was Mexican, Ted was sure of that.

"He says he doesn't have any nephews."

"Tell him I'm Eduardo Higuera. Named after my father, his little brother."

Kathy spoke to the old man.

"Tell him my dad went to California to look for him and found out he was MIA in Vietnam."

"He says he remembers a brother."

"Tell him my mom and dad spent their whole lives trying to find out what happened to him."

The old man squinted and leaned on his hoe. He spoke to Kathy.

"He says he has work to do. You can talk to him this evening."

"What's he doing? I'll help."

Kathy spoke to the old man and translated to Ted. "He's weeding his paddy."

235

The old man bent over and pulled some weeds from the bottom. He held them up and said something.

"He says this is what he's doing. He doesn't care if you wait, help, or leave."

"C'mon, kids." Ted dropped his backpack and helmet. "Let's get to work."

The four waded into the water and began pulling weeds. Every now and then the old man shouted warnings or instructions.

The day went quickly. Ted's back cried out in pain long before the sun set.

The old man spoke to Kathy.

"He says that we've done a week's worth of work today. We are welcome in his home."

"Ka-ching." Ted pumped his fist in the air. "Let's go."

FROM THE OUTSIDE, Gino's hooch looked no different from the dozen or so other hooches in the village. Built on four-foot-tall bamboo pilings, it had a wooden floor and stout bamboo poles holding up the thatched roof. The walls were covered with thatch as well.

The hooches surrounded a communal well and fire pit. People returning from the fields filled the open area.

"Come," Gino said in Vietnamese, waving his open hand toward his hut.

"Ask him why he doesn't speak English," Ted told Kathy.

Kathy and Gino spoke for a moment.

"He says he doesn't remember much English. He hasn't spoken it in fifty years."

"Shit." Ted turned to Gino. "*Requerda Español?*"

"*Sí, un poquito.*"

Hope stepped forward. "*Tio Gino, Soy Esperansa, tu sobrina.*"

Gino's face lit up and he opened his arms. Hope ran to hug him.

"What did she say, Kathy?" asked Chris.

Kathy just shrugged.

"She told him she was his niece," Ted said. "Apparently, he's happy to meet her."

Gino led them into his hooch. A smiling Vietnamese woman greeted them with bows. Kathy introduced them around.

"This is Minh, Gino's wife," Kathy explained.

The other three Americans offered their greetings.

The inside of the hooch was sparse. It consisted of a single room with a fire pit in the middle. There was a hole in the roof to let out the smoke.

A padded area covered with silk blankets was obviously the bed. In one corner a wooden rocking chair sat next to a small table. Cushions were scattered around on the floor.

"Uncle, we came to return you to the U.S.," Ted said in Spanish.

Gino waved to the cushions and bade the visitors to sit. "It is very good to meet you and my niece."

"You were a POW. How did you get here?" Hope asked.

Gino turned to her. "I was captured on a mission in North Vietnam. I was shot up pretty bad." Gino rubbed the long scar on the left side of his face. "They took us to a hospital. Minh was just a girl then. She took care of us, Gunnar and me. When we were well, they took us to a POW camp. Minh followed us." He reached out and took Minh's hand.

Minh must not have any idea what they were talking about, but she took Gino's hand and smiled into his eyes.

"She took care of us. Brought us food, did our wash. Then one day, she came with the camp commandant. They pulled me out of my cell and marched me to the commandant's office. I had to sign a lot of papers there. I had to pledge that I would never raise a hand against what was to become my adopted country."

Gino was silent for a long moment. His eyes twinkled; his mouth turned up into a slight smile. He closed his eyes and obviously returned to his youth.

"What's he saying?" Chris asked.

"He's telling us how he came to be here," Ted replied and translated for Chris and Kathy.

"I was paroled to Minh's father," Gino went on. "We came here to live with her family. Life has been good for me. After the war, we managed to build a good life. I made friends. We had children. They had children. There is nothing more I could ask for."

"But you have family in America," Hope cut in. "My papa is dead, but Mama is still there. You have a brother and two sisters in Mexico. You have lots of cousins and nephews."

Gino stroked his long, Vietnamese style beard. "I don't know those people. I have been perfectly happy here for fifty years."

"But, Uncle," Ted said, "they will welcome you with open arms. They will treat you as a hero. The whole country will treat you as a hero. Did you know you won the Congressional Medal of Honor? I'm sure the Secretary of Defense himself will present it to you. Maybe the president."

"I don't care about your medals. I have become Vietnamese. I have family here. Minh and I have three children and eight grandchildren."

Ted couldn't sit still. He rose and paced the room. "They could come with you. I'm sure we could get them out. Wouldn't you like your grandchildren to grow up in America? Have access to an American education?"

Gino's eyes followed Ted as he walked back and forth.

"Why do they need an American education? They have everything they need here. They have family, friends, good food and a home. They will grow up and marry other villagers and lead a happy life. They won't be exposed to the toxic American lifestyle."

Ted blew out a long breath. He closed his eyes and slowed his breathing. "We came half-way around the world to find you. You must come home with us."

"Nephew, I am honored that you have sought me out. I am flattered that you care about an old man. I don't have much time left on this planet. I choose to spend it here, with my family, my friends, in my country."

3 0

JUST DESSERTS — HANOI

The team spoke hardly a word as they trudged through the countryside to the first village to rendezvous with Giang.

From there, Giang led them back to civilization.

The first thing Kathy did when they arrived in Hanoi, was call Huong. She got no answer. She left text messages, but they weren't returned.

Giang took them to Kathy's cousin's house. A somber mood prevailed among the Americans.

"What could have happened to Huong? Why isn't she answering?" Kathy asked no one in particular.

THE NEXT MORNING Giang showed up with a melancholy look on his face. "I have news, and none of it is good."

Ted put down his teacup. "What's going on?"

"First of all, your friend Huong has disappeared. No one has seen her or heard from her."

Kathy gasped.

"I have worked my connections. I talked to a helicopter pilot who works for the secret police."

The four Americans just stared at him.

"He says," Gian went on, "that he recently flew a flight with dissidents on board –"

Kathy interrupted, "But Huong isn't a dissident. She's Colonel's Bao's niece."

"—He says they flew the young people far out over the ocean and pushed them out of the chopper."

"Oh, my God." Kathy's hands flew to her cheeks.

Hope's eyes watered and tears flowed down her face.

"What happened to them?" Ted asked. "Was Huong among them?"

"There were no survivors. They were handcuffed when they were pushed overboard from two thousand feet up."

"Shit." Ted kicked at the dirt floor and pressed for an answer again. "Was Huong with them?"

"He wasn't sure. He didn't see who his passengers were and didn't have a manifest."

"It wasn't the first time he made such flights. He knows that he has to keep his eyes and mouth shut if he wants to live to see his grandchildren."

"Crap." Chris lowered himself onto a cushion. "We know what they're capable of. We need to find out if Huong was one of the victims."

"She was," Ted said. "And Colonel Bao ordered it. There's no doubt in my mind."

"But his own niece?" Hope asked. "He wouldn't do that to family."

"The man's a megalomanic. He'll strike out at anything that threatens him. For some reason, he seems to think we're a threat." Ted turned to Kathy. "He lumps his niece in with us because she's your friend."

"Oh, God, I got her killed." Kathy shook with sobs.

Ted put an arm around Kathy and held her tight. "This isn't your fault. It's that madman, Bao. We've got to bring him to justice."

Kathy threw her arms around Ted's neck, snuggled into his shoulder, and wept.

"You know that'll never happen," Chris said. "He owns the secret police." Chris kicked the cushions on the floor. "Even if charges were brought against him, the witnesses would simply disappear. He's too high up in the government. He's untouchable."

"Hell no." Fire lit Ted's eyes. "That bastard has to pay for this."

A silence hung in the room until Giang spoke again. "That's not all. It gets worse."

"What the fuck could be worse?" Ted asked.

"Your exit visas have all been cancelled," Giang said. "You can't leave the country legally."

"My God," Hope said. "How will we get home?"

"I have made arrangements." Giang looked at the floor. "You will follow the same trail that Chun and Gunnar took. We will sneak you into Cambodia. There you can go to the U.S. Embassy and arrange for your own transport."

Hope let out a sigh.

"Great, when do they leave?" Ted asked.

"Hold on there, *hermano*," Hope said. "What do you mean 'they'?"

"You three go on ahead." Ted clenched his fist. His face turned red. "I have unfinished business here."

"No," Kathy said. "You must leave with us."

"Ted, you know that if you stay, I stay," Chris said. "I've never cut out on you."

"No. I need you to get the women out. I need to know they're safe."

"You're absolutely nuts." Hope pulled herself to her full height and puffed out her chest. With hands on hips she added, "We're not leaving without you. What you're planning is suicide. But if you stay, we stay."

Ted moved to the door and stared out. He looked at his friends. "You have to go. I can't do what I have to do knowing you're at risk. You need to leave so that I can finish this."

"I know that look in his eyes," Chris said. "He's made up his mind. There's nothing that we can do to change it."

"Teddy, no –" Hope shrieked.

Chris pulled her back. "Hope, he has to do this. We need to let him. I have to get you and Kathy out of the country."

"Not me." Fire flashed in Kathy's eyes. "I stay." Her voice strengthened between the sobs. "Huong was my best friend. I got her into this. Ted's a foreigner here. He doesn't know the language, the people, the culture. He wouldn't last a day here by himself. If he's going ahead with his crazy plan, whatever it is, I need to stay and keep him out of trouble."

"Absolutely not." Ted flung his head back to get the hair out of his eyes. "You need to go. I can't do what I have to do if you're here."

"You can't do it if I'm *not* here. I don't believe in revenge or killing, Ted, but I can't leave you alone in a strange land."

Ted was silent.

"It's settled then. Giang will get Chris and Hope out, and we'll stay and attend to business." Kathy's words had the air of finality.

Chris and Hope left with Giang. Ted sat on a cushion and stared into space. *What do I do? I can't just walk up and kill him. But no one ever deserved killing more. I'm not a killer. What would Cat do?*

He knew damn good and well what his erstwhile partner would do. She had cold bloodedly pulled the trigger on people that the justice system couldn't touch.

"Ted," Kathy laid a hand on his shoulder. "I made some calls. I got Bao's address."

"Umph." Ted broke out of his reverie and looked at Kathy. "Are you sure you're up for this? It's not going to end nicely."

"Somebody has to keep you honest."

Ted rose to his feet and gently pulled her to him. He put his arms around her and buried his head in her neck.

They hugged for a long moment, then Kathy stepped back. "We've got to get going if we want to beat rush-hour traffic."

Beat rush-hour traffic. It sounds like she's just planning a trip to the mall. "Okay, let's suit up." He reached for his CAT suit.

"Not a good idea. We should just dress casually so we don't stand out. You can't catch a cab if you're invisible. We'll suit up when we get there."

Ted nodded. "Okay but replace your batteries first. We don't want to run them dead in the middle of a mission." He carefully checked his backpack. *All good.* "Let's go."

THEY WANDERED through the back streets until they came to a main thoroughfare. Kathy flagged down two motorbike taxis and they took a wild ride to the high-rent district.

Bao's home stood out among the row of mansions. After the taxi drivers drove off, the cloud of blue smoke hung in the air, choking Ted, he led the way into the forest surrounding Bao's property.

In a small clearing, Ted stopped. "Let's change here." Ted took off his backpack and slung it to the ground.

Kathy whipped off her T-shirt and dropped her jeans.

Ted admired her thin body with subtle curves. *Jesus Christ. You're the least modest woman I ever met.* Ted stripped down. *Then again maybe it's just because you're so confident in yourself.*

They both wiggled into their CAT suits and put on the helmets.

Ted went through the checklist to make sure all systems worked. He turned off the GPS so there was no record of their movements should someone ever tap into their systems.

Winding their way through the jungle in invisible mode, they came to a clear area behind Bao's house. A huge lawn surrounded the building.

You built a killing field around your house. I wonder what kind of security you have?

"Oh, my God," Kathy said, staring up at the mansion.

Three stories tall with a basement that opened to the sloping lawn, it was built from bright white marble with a red tile roof. Tall and thin, the edifice looked as if it grew out of the ground.

Gleaming white columns held up the balcony surrounding the second floor. A gentle stream flowed near the building crossed by a stone bridge, with white wrought-iron railings.

"Jesus Christ." Ted caught his breath. "You'd expect Mr. Rourke to pop up saying, 'Welcome to Fantasy Island.'"

They crossed the lawn like two ghosts. Ted's head constantly swung back and forth, looking for threats even though his helmet had a threat detector built in.

A red light flashed, and an image of a guard armed with an AK-47 and a leashed German Shepard appeared on his HUD.

"Threat detected, Ted," Lilly said.

"Crap."

Ted saw a guard and dog coming around the house.

The dog sniffed the air and pulled at the leash. The Vietnamese man dropped to one knee and spoke softly to the dog.

"What're we going to do?" Kathy's high pitched voice came through Ted's helmet.

"Freeze." The dog could smell them, but what would happen when it couldn't see them?

The guard released the dog from its leash. The dog ran

snarling across the grass toward the two Americans. The guard trotted behind.

The dog charged at Ted and Kathy as if it could see them.

Kathy stood frozen. Ted reached for his silenced pistol.

"NO, TED!"

The dog lunged at Ted. He managed to get off a shot. the soft thwpp sound went unheard by the guard. The dog howled and barreled into Ted. A hundred pounds of flying dog took Ted to the ground.

The dog whined and nipped at the dart in its chest.

"TED, NO! You didn't shoot the dog."

Ted rolled the whining dog off him. "I just tranqed him. He'll be all right."

The dog went silent.

In the instant that all this happened, the guard came running to his dog's aid. Not understanding what happened, he unslung his rifle and flipped off the safety.

Ted calmly shot him with a dart.

The guard grunted and collapsed to the ground.

"Help me hide them," Ted said, as he grabbed the guard under his arms and dragged him toward the woods.

"That was close," Kathy said as she dragged the dog.

"Remind me to tell Allison," Ted said, "To incorporate some sort of odor destroyer in the next release."

They quietly strode across the lawn.

They circled the perimeter looking for an easy entrance point. A carefully maintained garden surrounded the back of the house. Ted crept up to the French doors and tried the latch.

"It's open. Come on."

Kathy darted up the steps and through the doors. Ted silently closed them.

They were in a room with a light-colored tile floor, the walls paneled in rich teak. An ornately carved bench rested against the wall under the windows just to the right of the doors. A beautiful teak table with a white porcelain bowl sat in front of it.

A huge, heavily framed door led to the next room. Intricate lattice work clung to the frame to make a circular entrance.

Ted and Kathy crept silently through the house, not encountering a soul. Ice crept up Ted's spine as they moved through the unoccupied house. It smelled as if evil lingered in the air.

They moved through a dining room that opened to the patio. Through a swinging door Ted saw a kitchen that would rival any five-star restaurant.

"Can you believe this shit?" he asked.

"How many dead bodies had to pile up so he could afford this?" Kathy replied.

The next room was a pool room with a massive table in the center and a bar against the wall. They moved on.

Ted tested the knob on the next door. It was locked. He put his helmet against the door and listened. Nothing.

He opened his backpack and took out a small electronic device with a coiled aluminum tube coming out of it. He dropped to his knees and looked up at Kathy. "Locked doors don't mean nuthin'."

He poked the tube under the door and switched on the box. Its cell phone-sized screen lit up with a picture of the inside of the room.

A teak desk, roughly the size of an aircraft carrier, dominated the room. Behind the desk sat a matching credenza. Ornately carved bookcases lined the walls.

As Ted swept the tube around the room. He spotted giant windows with sheer white curtains overlooking the gardens. Beneath the window a man sat motionless on a cushion.

"It's him. Bao's in there."

Ted got to his feet. "Check your weapons."

"No, Ted. You're not going to kill him. I came with you to stop you. You can't just take another human being's life."

"Not even if he so richly deserves it?"

"It's not our place to judge. We can capture him, take him out, and give him to the authorities."

"Yeah, in what world?" Ted pulled his lock-pick kit from a hip pocket. "Let's just pay Mr. Bao a little visit."

"Ted —" Kathy whispered as he opened the door.

COLONEL BAO SAT ON A CUSHION, facing the garden, but he didn't see. His mind was in turmoil. Yes, he ordered Huong's death, and yes, she was family. But he had to. She was a threat to his empire.

Those damn Americans. It's their fault. If they had never come here, none of this would have happened.

Images of the Americans flowed through his mind. But it was the short, dark one that kept coming back. Why this one? What was special about him?

True, he cost Bao millions of dollars breaking up his drug exporting to Mexico, but there was something else about him.

Bao focused his hatred on the dark one. Higuera had to die. He had to pay for this.

His mind made up, he started to rise, but heard the door opening. He spun to see who entered. No one. The door closed by itself.

Movement. He sensed movement in the room. But there was no one there.

"Colonel Bao," a voice came from out of nowhere. "It's time to pay the piper."

Bao tried to get up, but something shoved him back down on his cushion.

He reached for the gun in a drawer in the side table.

The drawer slammed shut. "Yow." He pulled away his crushed fingers.

"There's no place you can go that I can't follow." There was the voice again.

Was this the ghost of one of his ancestors?

"Who are you? What did I do?"

"What did you do?" The voice laughed. "What didn't you do? You killed your own niece. You're up to your ears in drugs. You're ruining countless lives. Killing countless people."

A pair of angry brown eyes floated above Bao.

"Who are you? What do you want?"

"I'm the angel of death. It's time for you to pay for your crimes. I'm here to avenge Huong."

"No." Bao rose to his feet. "Not Huong. She's alive. She's just away on a vacation. She always runs off to foreign countries without telling anyone."

Someone slapped his face, hard. He tumbled to the floor.

"You lying sack of shit."

Someone kicked Bao in the ribs. "Yaooooo . . . "

Bao lay on the floor, gasping for breath. "You'll, never ... get. . . away... with ... this."

"You will never get away with killing Huong," the voice said.

In front of Bao's eyes, a man materialized. Behind him another. No, this was a woman.

Bao caught his breath. "You will never get away with this," he repeated.

"You've gotten away with your shit for way too long."

TED PULLED the experimental pistol from its holster. He popped out the blue magazine and replaced it with a red one.

"Ted, no. You can't." Kathy reached for his arm. "We need to let the justice system handle this."

"Justice system." Ted laughed. "There is no justice system in this country. Men like Bao always get away with it."

What to do? He finally had Bao at his mercy. *I'm not a killer. I can't just shoot you in cold blood. But you can't be allowed to infest this country, this planet, for another day.*

"No court in Vietnam is going to convict him."

"Ted —"

Ted aimed the gun and pulled the trigger.

Bao screamed and grabbed his right knee.

"That's for Huong, you piece of shit."

Ted fired a second shot. Bao's left knee flew apart.

"I'm not going to kill you. I want you to suffer more than that. I'm going to fix it so that you can never do this again." He fired a third shot.

The nine-millimeter bullet slammed into Bao's left shoulder. Flesh and bone splattered the windows.

"Noooo," Bao shouted, crying in pain. Tears ran down his cheeks.

"Ted, stop." Kathy pulled at him. "You've done enough."

Ted shook her off.

"This is for all the misery you've spread across the country." Ted fired a fourth shot.

Bao's right shoulder shattered.

Bao lay on the floor, bleeding from all four wounds, crying out in anger and pain.

"I expect you to put the money you made back into the community. Build schools. Feed the hungry. Build hospitals."

Bao looked up at him.

"No, I'm not going to kill you, but just remember how easy we got to you. If you ever participate in illegal activities again, I'll know. Next time I won't be so lenient."

That's it. I couldn't kill him. That's not who I am.

The End

POSTSCRIPT

I hope you enjoyed reading Ted's latest adventure. It was joyous and sorrowful writing it in that it took me back to the time of my youth. We were young, full of energy, and going to change the world. As I look back now, we did change the world but I'm afraid not in a good way. I fear that we are leaving the world in worse shape for our succeeding generations that we found it.

Reviews are the lifeblood of independent writers. The more reviews we get, the more Amazon and others promote the book. If you want to see more Ted Higuera adventures, a review would go a long way towards allowing me to write more books. If you liked the book, I ask you to write a review of *Back to Vietnam* on Amazon.com, Goodreads or wherever you go for your book information. Thank you so much, it means the world to me. If you didn't like the book, then please disregard this paragraph.

I'd love to hear your comments and criticisms. Who knows, maybe some of your ideas will appear in a future Ted Higuera novel (As a matter of fact, Ted's previous book, *Cyberwarfare,* was suggested by a reader). To contact me click here or use the Contact Penn form on my web site at www.pennwallace.com.

Ted will take a sabbatical for a while. My next book, tentatively named *The Pirate and the Princess*, will soon appear on Amazon's Kindle Vella. We'll see how that works. I have a new Catrina Flaherty mystery in the works, and a semi-biographical historical novel about my great-grandfather in the Civil War.

Keep track of the progress of their next adventures on my website at www.pennwallace.com. Better yet, sign up for my readers' list and you'll get my monthly newsletter with all my latest progress, book recommendations, giveaways, and more. Sign up at http://pennwallace.com/sign-up-page.html.

For now, if you liked this story, you can browse my other books and short stories at http://www.pennwallace.com/index.html.

Thank you very much for reading my book. I hope you enjoy my other works and in those immortal words of Dean Martin, "Keep those cards and letters coming in."

Pendelton C. Wallace
January 21, 2023
San Diego, California

ACKNOWLEDGMENTS

First of all, I need to thank the members of my authors' critique group: David Larson, Mike Gibbs, Christina Buffington, Marla Anderson, and all the rest of you who've come and gone. They've suffered through the whole manuscript with me at least twice and made many suggestions that I've incorporated throughout the book. Thank you.

Rebecca Poole designed the cover for this book. She did her customary outstanding job of taking an idea and bringing it to life.

I would like to thank my editor, Larry Edwards. He did an above and beyond the call of duty job.

Donna Rich was my proofreader. If there are any errors left in this book, they are wholly my fault.

And, of course, I need to thank my dear friend Rick Lakin for formatting the book for publication.

Mike Gibbs, a retired San Diego police officer and former Green Beret, was my mentor and helper in shaping the Vietnam scenes. He corrected my errors and helped me write the battles as they happened.

I also want to thank the Vietnam veterans and Vietnamese people who I interviewed, too many to mention by name, who gave me a sound footing for understanding the country and the war.

I must thank my beta readers who saw the first draft of the manuscript and helped me smooth out the rough edges. You know who you are.

I also want to give a big shout out to my Advanced Readers. They put the finishing touches on the book and provided reviews on launch day.

I have to thank Mama. She's been in my corner from the beginning. She encouraged me when the night seemed darkest. I would not be publishing my tenth book without her. We just celebrated her ninety-eighth birthday. *Muchas gracias*.

And finally, I have to thank you, dear reader, especially those of you who have taken the time to write to me with your thoughts and comments. Without patrons, artists don't last very long. The fact that you read and enjoy what I write drives me onward. Like Thomas Jefferson, I believe that a free society must read to maintain its freedom. You are all freedom fighters.

Pendelton C. Wallace
January 23, 2023
San Diego, California

AUTHOR'S NOTE

Back to Vietnam is based on real events. In real life, an American GI was captured by the VC, sent to a North Vietnamese POW camp. For some reasons unknown the North never reported the prisoner and did not repatriate him at the end of the war. The Department of Defense listed him as Missing In Action (MIA).

Fifty years later, an American reported in Hanoi on another story hear rumors of this American prisoner still being held. He followed the story 'til the end and found the missing GI. I read the story in the newspapers and knew it had to be a Ted Higuera Thriller. I tried to follow the facts as carefully as I could, but as befits a work of fiction, I inserted my own characters and some of the characters in the book are an amalgamation of the real life people.

To paraphrase the old *Dragnet* TV show, the story you have just read is true, the names have been changed to protect the stupid.

I hope you enjoy the Ted Higuera Series. If you like Ted's stories, you need to read the Catrina Flaherty Mysteries too. You may have noticed that Catrina was absent from *Back to Vietnam*, *although she is mentioned*. That's because she's up to her neck looking for a serial killer in Panama. I hope you will check out *The Panama Murders*.

I'd love to hear from you. I've already gotten a couple of ideas for future books from readers like you. I've also had several people point out proof-reading errors that I correct and publish in future editions of my books. Most of all, I get praise from people who have been to the locations I write about. I'm already hearing from Vietnam War Veterans and so far, the reception has been good.

I also get a lot of questions. Why did Ted do this? Was Chris really thinking about that? I'd love to hear your thoughts and I promise to answer each one of your emails.

You can contact me from my web site, www.pennwallace.com, using the Contact Penn tab or email me at penn@pennwal lace.com. I'd love to hear from you.

Pendelton C. Wallace
January 23, 2023
San Diego, California

ALSO BY PENDELTON C. WALLACE

CATRINA FLAHERTY MYSTERIES

Mirror Image (Catrina Flaherty Mystery 1)

Based on a real-life tragedy, *Mirror Image* is a heart-stopping tale of horrific abuse.

Female PI Catrina Flaherty tackles one of her most difficult cases. Cat specializes in women's issues: infidelity, messy divorces, spousal abuse, sexual harassment, etc. But her newest client, Mandy Alcott, has an unusual problem; her abusive husband is the chief of police.

Who you gonna call when your abuser is The Law?

Cat Flaherty.

Murder Strikes Twice (Catrina Flaherty Mystery 2)

When her daughter dies in a tragic accident and the daughter's husband's second wife does the same, what is Eleanor Johnson to think? The police have ruled both cases accidents and closed them, but something doesn't feel right. Is it possible to believe that two tragic deaths are mere coincidence, or was something more sinister at play? Who's Eleanor gonna call?

Cat Flaherty.

Murder Strikes Twice, the second book in the Catrina Flaherty Mysteries, is based on an actual case.

When Cat starts looking into the Barrett Case, something smells rotten. She and her team scour Seattle for clues as the pieces start falling into place, but can she make a case that the D.A. will take to court? Did Murder Strike Twice or will Brody Barrett get away with killing both of his wives?

Catrina is known for administering vigilante justice. Will Brody finally have to pay for his sins?

The Chinatown Murders (Catrina Flaherty Mystery 3)

WARNING: This book contains graphic sexual violence. Not intended for younger readers.

Based on a true story.

Someone is raping women working at massage parlors in Seattle's China Town. He selects his victims because they are undocumented aliens. Their families can't go to the police or they risk deportation.

Now he has escalated to murder.

Who you gonna call?

Cat Flaherty.

The Man leads Catrina on a danger-fraught chase through the ancient streets of Chinatown in a race against time. Neither Catrina, nor her ex-lover, Detective Sergeant Tom Brennen, can stop the monster as the body count piles up.

With a shock ending that you'll never predict, the latest Cartrina Flaherty Mystery is a page burner.

The Panama Murders (Catrina Flaherty Mysteries Book 4)

BASED ON A TRUE STORY

Warning: This description contains a spoiler from one of Cat's previous novels.

People on a remote Panamanian island are disappearing, and the local police are incompetent.

Who you gonna call?

Cat Flaherty.

When the love of Seattle PI Catrina Flaherty's life turns out to be a serial killer, she turns him over to the police and walks away from her business, home, and friends. She slinks off to Panama to recover from her broken heart.

Staying with Suzanne, a friend from the police academy, she meets colorful characters and observes the sometime bizarre lifestyle of the ex-pats. She is enchanted by the beauty and the wildlife, but when people start dying, it's obviously the work of a serial killer. Cat is sucked back into her role as an investigator and the killer soon has her in his sights.

Can Cat discover the identity from a host of persons of interest before he gets her?

THE TED HIGUERA THRILLERS

The Inside Passage *(Ted Higuera Series Book 1)*

Somewhere on Canada's Inside Passage, terrorist plot to blow up a cruise ship filled with celebrities and VIP's. Ripped from today's headlines, a group of Canadian-born terrorist plan to bring their war to the Western Hemisphere.

Ted Higuera and his friends stumble upon the al-Qaeda plot and the clock starts ticking.

Can Ted and his friends act in time to save the thousands of people aboard the *Star of the Northwest* or will the terrorists take them out of the picture?

HACKER for Hire *(Ted Higuera Series Book 2)*

If Clive Cussler had written *Ugly Betty*, it would be *Hacker for Hire*.

Hacker for Hire, a suspense novel about corporate greed and industrial espionage, is the second book in a series about computer security analyst Ted Higuera and his best friend, paralegal Chris Hardwick.

When you're already in the top 1% of the country's money makers, how much is enough?

Ted and lovely PI, Catrina Flaherty, are led deep into Seattle's Hi-Tech jungle as they stalk a killer. But the killer is also hunting them. Can they find the killer before the killer finds them?

This is the introduction to Cat Flaherty. If you're a fan of hers, you have to read this book.

THE MEXICAN CONNECTION *(Ted Higuera Series Book 3)*

In *The Mexican Connection*, the third book in the Ted Higuera series, Ted and Chris are lured to Mexico by an old nemesis. They are dragged into Mexico's drug wars and have to confront the corruption of Mexico's law enforcement. They meet a colorful cast of characters as they search from border towns to the cosmopolitan Mexico City to ancient Aztec ruins.

In the meantime, Cat is in Mexico on a mission of her own. Her client, a Seattle housewife, is thrown into jail when her drug-dealing husband disappears, leaving her holding the bag.

You will meet old friends, make new ones and encounter new villains as our heroes cut a wide swath through our neighbor to the south. Throw in a magical Jaguar and an Aztec god and you have a rollicking adventure tale.

BIKINI BARISTAS (TED HIGUERA Series Book 4)

Bikini Baristas is a tale of Dick Randall, the owner of a chain of bikini barista stands in the Seattle area and Clayton Johnson-White, a teenage kid who thinks he's smarter than the rest of the world.

The story begins when Dick's pickup truck is discovered burned-out in the California desert. What happened to him? Did he fake his death to escape his sleazy past or did the past catch up with him?

Catrina Flahery and Ted Higuera are hired by his wife to find out what happened.

To get away from his trailer-trash life, Clayton drops out of school and runs away into the woods of Camano Island. He breaks into vacation homes and steals what he needs.

The case is handed to Ted's best friend, Chris Hardwick, his first grown-up lawyer case.

What do these two cases have in common? In the end, they come together with the force of two colliding freight trains.

THE CARTEL STRIKES Back *(Ted Higuera Series Book 5)*

. . .

RIPPED FROM TODAY'S HEADLINES, the world's most wanted criminal, Mexican drug lord, El Pozolero, escapes from prison and vows revenge on the man who sent him there: Ted Higuera.

Ted finally gets up the nerve to propose to Maria. What happens next will take your breath away. As Maria runs away to Mexico and El Pozolero moves in, the body count soars.

The Cartel Strikes Back ends with a shock you won't see coming.

Cyberwarfare

Ripped from today's headlines. Readers of Tom Clancy, Michael Connelly, Michael Mather, and Daniel Suarez will love Ted Higuera.

Terrorists launch and all-out cyber-attack on the United States. Ted Higuera is inexorably drawn into the plot, making him a suspect.

Ted Higuera, son of Mexican immigrants, is a talented cyber-security analyst who's earned the nickname of "Hacker for Hire." He and his posse dig deep into the Dark Net to discover who is trying to bring the United States to its knees.

Unfortunately, the cyber-terrorists know Ted is on their trail and set him up to take the fall.

Can he stay out of the grasp of Homeland Security and discover who is behind this mysterious attack?

Join Ted and company as they negotiate the twisted path that leads them to the bad guys.

You won't be able to put this one down.

WARNING: There are graphic scenes of torture in this book.

OTHER BOOKS BY PENDELTON C. WALLACE

Blue Water & Me, Tall Tales of Adventures With My Father

Blue Water & Me is a high-adventure true story of author Penn Wallace's magical first summer fishing with his father, Blue Water Charlie, off the coast of Mexico at age eleven.

CHRISTMAS INC.
Amazon.com's #1 bestselling political satire.

What would happen if Santa decided to go public and sell shares of Christmas on the NASDAQ? What would happen to the elves if he outsourced toy making to China? What if he was forced to take a government bail out?

WARNING: This is not a children's book. Exposure to children under 12-years old may cause the child to stop believing in Santa Claus or take a cynical view of Christmas.

ABOUT THE AUTHOR

Pendelton Wallace is the author of three number one bestselling novels, *Christmas Inc, Hacker for Hire,* and *The Chinatown Murder.* He is the author of the Ted Higuera Series, and the Catrina Flaherty Mysteries.

If Chevy Chase had played Indiana Jones, he would be Penn Wallace. Penn has a thirst for adventure, but nothing ever seems to go exactly as planned.

Penn graduated from the University of Oregon (Go Ducks!) and has had three careers. He owned and operated two restaurants and worked for several major chains. In 1990, he went back to school, got his MBA in Information Systems and embarked on a new life.

After his wife died in 2010, Penn lost all interest in work. He left his career as a software engineer and bought a big old sailboat. He spent the next two years restoring the vessel.

In the fall of 2012, he set sail for the warm blue waters of Baja California in his 56-foot sailboat, the *Victory,* picking up a gorgeous blonde and a couple of Great Danes along the way. You may read an account of this adventure on his blog at www.pennwallace.com. This is when Penn started his third career, as a writer.

Penn resides in San Diego where he spends time at the beach and enjoys the lovely winter weather.

You may contact Penn at http://www.pennwallace.com/contact-penn.html and visit his web site at www.pennwallace.com.

www.ingramcontent.com/pod-product-compliance
Lightning Source LLC
Chambersburg PA
CBHW072208170626
46813CB00003B/844